"I've missed you," he said, his voice low. "More than I realized."

As he began to lower his head, Ellie felt her eyes flutter shut.

Gently he placed a small series of nibbling kisses along the lower rim of her mouth, undemanding, soft and inquisitive.

With a moan of surrender, she eagerly rose on tiptoe to press her body closer to his. Her action caused him to tug her closer to his body and she became acutely aware of her breasts pressed against his hard chest.

She inhaled a swift breath. There was nothing innocent about the feel of his arousal, strong and unyielding as it pressed against her belly.

"God, Ellie…you taste so good. Your mouth is like honey," he told her with a catch in his voice. He bent back down to recapture her lips, wrapping his hands around her waist and pulling her impossibly closer to his big, hard body.

Arching her body fully into his, on fire from his talented tongue, Ellie tunneled her fingers through his hair.

"Dr. Eleanor Crandall, you're wanted at the front!"

And just like that, the sound of her father's voice right outside the door brought Ellie's eyes wide open.

Books by Kimberly Kaye Terry

Kimani Romance

Hot to Touch
To Tempt a Wilde
To Love a Wilde
To Desire a Wilde

KIMBERLY KAYE TERRY

Kimberly Kaye Terry's love for reading romances began at an early age. Long into the night she would stay up with her Mickey Mouse night-light on, until she reached The End, praying she wouldn't be caught reading what her mother called "those" types of books. Often she would acquire her stash of "those" books from beneath her mother's bed. Ahem. To date she's an award-winning author of fourteen novels in romance and erotic romance, has garnered acclaim for her work and happily calls writing her full-time job.

Kimberly has a bachelor's degree in social work, a master's degree in human relations and has held licenses in social work and mental health therapy in the United States and abroad. She volunteers weekly at various social-service agencies and is a long-standing member of Zeta Phi Beta Sorority, Inc., a community-conscious organization. Kimberly is a naturalist and practices aromatherapy. She believes in embracing the powerful woman within each of us and meditates on a regular basis. Kimberly would love to hear from you. Visit her at www.kimberlykayeterry.com.

To Desire a
WILDE

Kimberly Kaye Terry

KIMANI
ROMANCE

To my amazing daughter, who fills me with laughter and makes my days brighter. I love you, pooh!

KIMANI PRESS™

ISBN-13: 978-0-373-86209-2

TO DESIRE A WILDE

www.kimanipress.com

Printed in U.S.A.

Dear Reader,

There is nothing sexier or more emotionally charged than reaching for and holding on tight to a love you once thought unattainable—which is exactly what happens to the hero and heroine in my third installment of the Wilde in Wyoming series.

In *To Desire a Wilde,* sexy Shilah Wilde comes face-to-face with Ellie Crandall, the one woman he's never been able to get out of his mind—something that no one, least of all Ellie, ever knew. When she left Wyoming to pursue her career as a veterinarian, following in her father's footsteps, she swore she'd never return, despite the feelings she once had for Shilah. But now she's back, ten years later, and working for the USDA in a case against the Wilde Ranch. Despite doubts and questions, sparks fly and passions ignite. The hidden yearnings they once shared for each other blossom into a raging passion that sets the Wyoming Wilde Ranch and everything in its path ablaze.

I appreciate your support and will *always* do my best to deliver to you, my valued readers, emotionally charged stories filled with love, life and laughter...and red-hot, scalding passion!

Keep it sexy!

Kimberly

Chapter 1

Ellie's booted footsteps sank silently into the damp grass that separated the east stable from the closed corral. She stopped at the coral's locked gate and propped her arms along the fence and tilted her face upward.

The sun fell like magic against her upturned face. An unknowing smile tugged at the corners of her full lips as she drew in a deep, hungry breath.

It had been a long time since she'd been at the ranch. She blew out the breath and turned her attention to the lone corralled horse.

The female thoroughbred standing alone, isolated, was one of the Wilde Ranch's latest acquisitions, one that Nate Wilde, the oldest brother, had bought at a ranch near Cheyenne several months ago.

From her father, who was the veterinarian for the Wilde Ranch, Ellie knew they'd tried mating the

Arabian a few times with several of their top-quality quarter horses. However, they had quickly realized that although they'd managed to tame her, it hadn't been enough to allow her to tolerate another horse anywhere near her—at least not for mating.

She stood grazing in the middle of the corral, content to be left alone.

Ellie felt a certain empathy with the beautiful horse. She too found contentment in being alone.

After several minutes Ellie turned away and again lifted her face upward, shielding her eyes from the brightly glowing sun.

It was late spring, and nature had awakened from her winter sleep. The ranch was alive with noise from horses and cattle as well as sounds of men hard at work across the sprawling ranch.

Spring was mating and branding season for the cattle, and with a new venture into crossbreeding horses, it was a busy time at Wyoming Wilde. The men were also hard at work preparing for one of their largest auctions, to come in the fall, and a lot depended on this season.

The ranch had come a long way from the days when Jed Wilde had run the one hundred acre spread alone, trying to make ends meet. Now it was one of the most prosperous family-owned ranches in the country.

Ellie glanced around, remembering the many times she'd visited the ranch growing up, accompanying her father on his visits.

She'd always felt at home at Wyoming Wilde. As the only child of older parents, she'd been cosseted, protected—some would say overly protected—by both parents and outside of activities with them; the ranch had become a second home to her.

Ellie had come as a complete surprise to her mother, told long ago she couldn't have children. Because of that, her parents' tendency toward overprotecting her had made Ellie more content at home, curled up with a book or playing with the few animals her parents had on their own land.

With her love for animals, the ranch became her own haven. Only at the ranch did her father give her free rein to explore, allowing her to follow the ranchers around as they went about their duties. It was a place where she felt like any other child, playing, learning about the animals, without inhibition.

A bittersweet memory flooded her mind. It was also the place where part of that independence her parents had afforded her had been taken away.

She'd been young, only ten years old, not long after Jed Wilde had become a foster father for three young boys he'd later adopted.

Ellie had been riding one of the horses, alone, something she knew her father wouldn't approve of. But she had been so caught up in the sheer enjoyment of the warm day, riding with the wind rushing against her face, she hadn't realized she'd gone out so far, with no one around.

Voices calling out to her had caught up with her on the wind, and she'd stopped, glancing over her shoulder to see Jed Wilde and the three young boys riding with him.

Surprised, Ellie had spun around and startled the horse when she'd reined him around too fast. The horse had lost its footing and Ellie had come tumbling down. With her foot caught in the stirrup the panicked horse had dragged her several feet until the men had caught up with them and managed to free Ellie.

She didn't remember much after that. The searing pain radiating from her knee up the length of her thigh had made her so dizzy she'd passed out. She'd come in and out of consciousness, her father clutching her hand as Jed Wilde had driven them to the hospital.

When finally she'd awakened, it had been in a hospital bed, staring up into the worried face of a young boy.

She'd been confused, dazed and not sure where she was, or who the boy was staring down at her.

"It's…it's gonna be all right," he'd whispered.

Ellie had frowned, sniffing back tears. "What—" She'd stopped speaking, grimacing when she moved and a pain shot up her leg. "What happened?"

He'd touched her hand, holding it within his, his young face lined with worry. "You had an accident. But everything is gonna be okay. They fixed you up real good. Everything is gonna be okay," he said again, as though he didn't know what else to say to her.

Before Ellie could ask who he was, her parents, along with a nurse, had rushed into her room. Her mother ran to her side, and from her peripheral vision Ellie saw the boy step back, silently moving away and allowing her mother to take the hand he'd just held.

She'd learned that when she'd fallen from the horse, one foot had gotten caught in the stirrup. Unable to free herself, the horse had dragged her, and her knee had violently turned. During the traumatic chain of events she'd also suffered a concussion.

Upon her arrival at the hospital, unconscious, she'd had an MRI of her knee—the swelling had been so severe, they were unable to ascertain the extent of the damage. She'd suffered an ACL injury that would take years of therapy, and eventually surgery. The devastating news that her knee would never be the same and she'd have to wear a brace for years to regain her mobility had changed her life.

Although her knee had healed—better than the doctors had expected, in fact—there were times when her limp became more pronounced. But it was unnoticeable most of the time Her continual physical therapy, the brace she wore for years and sheer determination had seen to that.

Even as a girl Ellie had a determination that belied her young years. The pain that came with recovery she could deal with. It was the stares and looks of sympathy on the faces of her peers, and adults, that had left a scar deeper than the ones inflicted on her knee.

Already introverted, she had retreated even further into her shell. So her father had reluctantly allowed her to come back to the ranch, desperate to see his daughter return to being the happy child she'd been, before the accident.

At the ranch she was able to be free, no one looked at her with sympathy in their eyes as their glance would fall to her leg, supported by the brace. At Wyoming Wilde, the ranchers allowed her to work, encouraged her to and treated her like one of them.

At the ranch, the men…as well as Jed's young foster sons, treated her like anyone else, something she never forgot.

Especially one of the boys, in particular, the one whom she'd seen at the hospital, who'd taken her hand. Shilah Wilde.

The memory of Shilah Wilde replaced those of a more

painful nature. Although she'd been only a young girl, she remembered how his concern for her had affected her, the way he'd wiped away her tears and held her hand, even for that brief moment,.

Each of the boys had his own distinct personality. Nate, the oldest, took on the role of big brother, and had always seemed to be mature, despite his young age. Holt, the youngest brother, was the flirt, the one with the ready comeback.

But it was the middle brother, Shilah, whom Ellie had been drawn to.

He was quieter than his brothers, yet in his dark eyes there was a wealth of humor at times, sadness at others. She remembered her mother once commenting that Shilah had what the old people would call an "old soul."

Although she only saw him a handful of times during her visits to the ranch before her accident, she'd been aware that he'd been following her. Before the accident, she'd been too shy to call out to him, let him know that she knew he was following her.

Afterward, it had taken months before she'd garnered enough courage to do so. It wasn't long before their tentative friendship had blossomed into one Ellie had cherished.

He'd brought out a side of her that few besides her parents ever saw, especially after the accident. His ability to make her laugh, even when she didn't want to, was one that she never forgot.

And she'd never forgotten his impact on her.

"Ellie? Is that you?" A deep voice penetrated her thoughts, jerked her out of her memories. She spun around.

Shielding her eyes with her hand, Ellie watched as a large figure emerged from the cover of a newly budding magnolia tree. Slowly she backed up, until her back bumped up against the wood fence, her heartbeat increasing in tempo.

She knew she was safe at the ranch, as once, long ago, it had been like a second home to her. But now, everything…everyone, was so new to her, it was as though she were seeing the place for the first time.

Once the figure came into full view, Ellie drew in a breath, her mouth forming a perfect O of surprise. It couldn't be…

"Shilah?" she asked, her frown easing from her mouth as the figure came into full view.

"Hey, El…long time no see," he said, a slow smile hijacking the corner of his mouth, his voice deeper than she remembered.

She drew in a breath, her glance sliding over him as he stood several feet away.

Not only was his voice deeper than she remembered, but he was taller. At five foot eight, Ellie was used to being close to the same height as most men. In heels she was often taller. But as he drew closer, despite the high heels on her boots, she had to stretch her neck up to see into his face.

Oh, mercy… And *what* a face. He removed his Stetson and a soundless breath of appreciation escaped from her lips.

For a moment she stood still, their gazes locked. Once he removed his hat, she could see his face fully. Handsome was *much* too tame a description for him.

His skin was a natural light golden hue, due to his Native American heritage, reminding her of cream with a strong hint of sweet, decadent honey. High sculpted cheekbones, a narrow nose and square chin gave him the kind of looks that would make anyone stop and stare. The set of his features was perfect. His face could have been sculpted by a master artisan.

But it was his eyes that sent a deep shiver over her body, despite the warm day. Dark, slashing brows were set above deep-set chocolate-brown eyes, the thin ring of gold around the iris lending him an almost…predatory appearance.

Her glance slid to his mouth, where one corner was curved lightly in a half smile and everything… *feminine*…in Ellie went still. As he moved closer, she found herself rooted to the spot, unable to move.

Several steps more and he was standing a foot away from her. "You're home," he said, simply.

Before she could read the play of emotions that crossed his handsome face he'd reached over and pulled her close, tight against his body and into his once-familiar embrace.

Chapter 2

Once he released her, he pushed her away, running his glance over her.

Ellie's heart was still pounding out a ragged beat and she quelled the urge to place her hand in her hair to tuck imaginary strands back into the low chignon she wore at the base of her neck.

Shaken, she took a few steps away, when the boot of her heel caught on a piece of timber, turning her ankle and twisting her knee. She hissed, reached down and gingerly rubbed her knee.

Immediately he was there, next to her, grabbing her beneath the elbow to steady her.

"Are you okay?" Shilah asked, his warm hand cupped beneath her elbow.

Ellie bit back a curse. Of all the times for her to lose her balance—this was the one time she would give anything for it *not* to happen.

She shook her head, dismissing her clumsiness, hiding her grimace as well as her embarrassment.

"I'm fine…just clumsy," she said. "And I should have known better than to try and be cute by wearing these boots," she finished in self-mockery, laughing lightly and glancing up at him. As she looked into his handsome face, old ghosts reared and Ellie inwardly cringed, expecting to see sympathy in his dark eyes. That was something she couldn't take. Especially from Shilah.

"From where I stand, I'd have to say with all selfishness that a potential tumble was well worth it, considering what those boots do for your legs."

She wet her bottom lip, not sure what to say she was so shocked at his reply. She tugged the hem of her skirt down past her knee and glanced back up at him. Instead of the sympathy she dreaded to see lurking there, what she saw made her draw in a short breath.

She remembered how gorgeous he'd been as a young man, the way he'd look at her, a half smile on his sensual lips in response to something she'd said, sending her young heart thumping out of control. But now, standing before her, so tall that his broad shoulders blocked out the noontime sun's blazing rays, Stetson held loosely in his big hand…the man was devastating.

She drew in a breath, wetting the bottom rim of her lip. When his gaze followed her action, she swallowed and forced herself to look away.

"Are you okay?" he asked again, and she shook her head, the smile on her face shaky.

"I'm fine." When she pulled away slightly, after only a brief pause, he released his hold on her, allowing her to move away.

"So I see," he said, and her gaze flew to his again, her heartbeat hiccupping in her chest. In his enigmatic expression she was unable to determine if he meant the comment in any way besides the reference to her turning her ankle.

She smiled tightly and turned toward the horse in the corral.

"Dad says you and your brothers have started breeding racehorses," she said, in an attempt to get the conversation toward safer ground.

She felt his gaze on hers and held her breath, only releasing it when he turned toward the horse.

"Yeah, we've gone into breeding and crossbreeding. It's been going well for us. It was mainly Nate's idea, although we've been thinking about doing it for a while now," he said, and she nodded her head.

"Dad says you bought more land a couple of years ago," she both asked and stated.

"We did. Actually it was six years ago, after Dad died. It was part of the original land he'd purchased but had to sell in order to keep the ranch afloat years ago."

"Has he been...gone that long?" she shook her head.

The mention of Jed Wilde brought a look of sadness to Shilah's face. "Yeah, time has a way of going on, no matter what."

"Seems like yesterday he was out here with you... with all of us. Teaching us, sharing his love for the ranch," she said after a long moment, a reminiscent smile on her face. "Showing us how to brand a cow," she finished with a small laugh.

"Yeah, and I remember that only *too* well. When he

offered to let you brand one you had no problem. Did it like you'd been branding cows your whole life. But when my turn came around, I passed out," he said with a groan, and Ellie laughed outright.

"That's funny, huh?" he asked, and although his look was stern, she saw the humor lurking in his unique eyes.

"Yep, sure is," she quipped, unrepentant. "What was it Holt started calling you after that?" Ellie frowned, trying to remember the nickname.

"Sheila…Little Heifer Who Sleeps With Cows," he filled in, deadpan, and Ellie's laughter grew. "He shortened it to Sheila."

"Oh, my God, that was funny," she said around her laughter.

"I caught a lot of shit from my brothers about that. It was a long time before Holt stop referring to me by that name," he said, running a hand over the back of his neck, a humorous yet chagrined look on his handsome face, and a fresh wave of giggles assaulted Ellie.

"Of course, after that, Holt, the eternal funnyman, couldn't stop. When I sliced into my finger while we were slaughtering I was known as Sheila, Boy Who Spills His Guts," he said, and again, Ellie's laughter rang out. By the time he finished reminiscing about the various nicknames his brother had given him, she was swiping tears from her eyes.

"Why'd you leave, Ellie? Why'd you leave without saying goodbye?"

His question brought Ellie up short and her laughter died out. Slowly, she dragged her eyes up to meet his intense stare.

* * *

Shilah glanced down at Ellie, taking in the somber set of her features, and he cursed himself.

For a moment, she was the young girl he remembered from their childhood, particularly before her accident, when her carefree laughter would ring out on the wings of the wind as she played on the ranch.

Within several months of his calling the ranch home, Shilah had first glimpsed Ellie. It was her laughter that had brought him to the shed that held the horses. He'd watched as she'd fed the horse, petting and talking to it as though it understood what she was saying. Her love and natural affinity for the horse had reminded him of his life on the reservation and instantly made him curious about her.

He'd followed her without her knowledge as she'd taken the horse out for a ride.

He'd stayed out far enough behind that she hadn't been aware of him, yet he'd been able to watch her and it had set a pattern. Whenever she'd visit the ranch, while her father took care of the animals she'd go for one of her rides, and he'd find an excuse to leave without his brothers or foster father knowing.

He'd been set to follow her one day as she rode, but a call from Jed had made him turn around and head back home. It had been on that day that part of her laughter had been taken from her, a day he'd never forgotten.

The accident had been freakish and although he, his brothers and father weren't to blame, a part of Shilah had always faulted himself for her fall. Had he followed her that day, or at least told her father where she was, he could have somehow prevented the fall and the accident.

It had taken a long time after the accident before he had been able to forget the pain in her eyes when she'd glanced up at him. She'd looked so small in the hospital bed, the crisp white linens startling against her deep brown skin as she gazed up at him, pain and confusion in her light brown eyes.

It had taken even longer for him to finally get the nerve up to talk to her. By then, she was even more closed off, more introverted than he remembered, and any attempt at conversation was normally met with silence or at most a short reply before she'd make an excuse to turn and, favoring her uninjured leg, walk away.

His glance slid over her as she stood close to him, their gazes locked.

Eventually, she'd begun to thaw toward him, open up to him, allowing him to become what he'd learned was a small circle of people she trusted. Her visits to the ranch with her father increased, and whenever he knew she was coming, he took pains with his appearance, carefully keeping his friendship with Ellie from his brothers.

Not because he was afraid of the ribbing he'd no doubt get, but because their friendship was special to him, unlike any relationship he'd had with anyone else.

After graduating from high school and entering college, their time together was short. Between school and work, Shilah barely had time for much else. Life for Ellie became busy as well, with preparing for college and working in her father's office part-time, the two grew apart.

And then one day he came home and learned from her father that she'd decided to attend college out of state, and he hadn't seen her since. Yet he had never forgotten her, never forgotten how important she was to him, how her smile seemed to light up the room when she came in.

Never forgotten how much he loved her, even though they'd been so young.

His gaze ran over her, as she stood a few feet away from him.

She'd grown up a lot since those days. She no longer wore the brace she worn for years. His eyes went over the smooth, uninterrupted view of her long, brown legs. The hem of her skirt flirted just below knee level, and her high-heeled boots stopped at her shapely calves.

His gaze traveled back up the length of her body. The weather was warm and she wore a light sweater over her blouse, yet her full breasts pressed against the soft-looking fabric.

He forced his glance away.

A frown creased her forehead at his question. "I don't know why I left. I guess a part of me knew that if I stayed, I'd never experience life, in a way." She shrugged. "After the accident, my parents were always afraid for me. They never really allowed me to be…free." She halted. "That's as good a word as any, I suppose."

For a moment it appeared as though she'd been about to say something else, but she placed a small smile on her face and glanced back toward the penned horse.

Desperately wanting to replace the sad look in her eyes, and not wanting to delve too deeply into what else he saw, Shilah shifted the conversation. Soon she was laughing again over his exploits with his brothers.

Somehow during their conversation they'd ambled toward a nearby bench. He motioned for her to sit.

She glanced over the pasture before she turned to face him. One side of her mouth lifted in a small smile. Shilah's gaze settled over her features. The look on her face was serene, beautiful, content. It was an image that immediately lodged in his heart.

It was several minutes before she answered, and when she did the smile on her face was as enigmatic as her answer. And drew him to her, just as it had when they were young.

His glance fell to her hands as they rested in her lap. With one hand, she toyed with the fingers of the other, sliding her forefinger around and around in a circular pattern in the palm of the other hand.

"I guess I came home…" She paused, her hand movement stilling as her glance raked over his face, the look in her eyes one that sent his heartbeat thumping harshly against his chest. "Because, well, it was time."

Shilah barely refrained from reaching out and grasping her hand and tugging her toward him, silently wishing that part of her reason for returning home was because of him.

Chapter 3

Shilah strode into the sprawling, five-thousand-square-foot house he'd called home for nearly twenty years, withdrew his jacket and lifted his Stetson from his head, absently tossing both on the hallway table.

He sidestepped the ladder that rested against the wall near the laundry room, along with a variety of other building materials, making a mental note to remind his brothers to tell the construction crew to clean up after themselves when they broke for the day. If they didn't, he would be the first in line to duck and hide when Lilly came after them for "messing up my house."

Hopefully, the general mayhem and mess would soon be over, finishing the construction that would add two additional wings on the house to accommodate their growing family. Although their home was large enough now for everyone, with both of Shilah's brothers engaged, the decision had been made to add separate suites for them, for privacy.

The distant smell of lunch permeated the air, but there was no sign of Lilly or anyone else in the spacious kitchen. He glanced over at the antique grandfather clock in the foyer. It was almost time for Yasmine and the others to start preparing for dinner. But, as he hadn't eaten since breakfast, he couldn't wait for the others and made his way to the fridge. He withdrew a cold beer, and, twisting off the cap, he tipped his head back and allowed the bitter amber to slide down his throat.

"You do realize that it's not even four o'clock, huh, bro?"

Shilah knew it had to be too good to be true—that he might actually have a moment to himself alone, when he could think in private about the bombshell life had just thrown, in the way of Ellie Crandall.

He didn't bother turning to face his brother, but simply finished off his beer before placing the empty bottle on top of the marble counter near the fridge. Reluctantly he turned to face Holt.

As usual, a shit-eating grin was split across his youngest brother's face, and as usual Shilah ignored it, simply lifting a brow. "I'm sure it's five o'clock somewhere."

Holt nodded his head. "Yeah, guess you're right about that." Holt pushed away from the bar-style counter and walking farther into the kitchen.

Shilah moved to the side, to allow him to reopen the fridge. When he pulled out an assortment of sliced turkey and ham, along with a variety of toppings, Shilah's stomach rumbled in response.

Holt glanced over his shoulder, meeting his eyes. "You missed lunch too?"

"Yeah," Shilah answered. "Just got back from the south pasture. I was hoping Lilly left me a plate from lunch."

"Naw, Lil is resting. Ellie and the new kitchen girl did lunch today." He threw Shilah a forlorn look. "And Yaz didn't even make lunch for me. Guess my baby missed the memo."

Shilah raised a brow. "Which one was that?"

"You hungry?" he asked, and Shilah nodded his head.

After withdrawing two plates from the overhead cabinet, Holt went about deftly slicing tomatoes and pickles. "The one that says the way to a man's heart is through his stomach," he groused, and Shilah barked out a laugh.

Recently, Holt had become engaged to Yasmine Taylor, their housekeeper Lilly's niece. Although Lilly was much more than a housekeeper to the men, having been a part of the ranch before Shilah, Holt and Nate had arrived as foster kids.

Thinking back, Shilah had a hard time remembering when the woman wasn't a part of their lives, as she'd been more like a surrogate mother to Shilah and his two brothers from the time they were young.

Her niece Yasmine had been a part of the ranch for nearly as long, coming to live with them when she was a child, as well. Soon after graduating high school she'd left, and her visits to the ranch after that had been few and far between. She'd come home last month to help Lilly recover after her knee-replacement surgery and…

Shilah glanced at his brother, holding back a laugh

when he bit out a curse after slicing into his finger, again grumbling about his woman and her neglect.

…And that was all she wrote, Shilah finished the thought. Penthouse—the nickname Holt had been given when he'd played pro ball, known for changing his women as often as most men changed their shorts—had fallen and fallen hard. And Yasmine had fallen just as hard, the pair inseparable since their engagement. When Holt wasn't working, he could be found with Yasmine, helping her as she planned the opening of her own catering business, as well as meeting with producers for a cooking show that would begin taping in the fall.

"Grab some bread. Yaz and I made some rye last night," Holt said, making a sound with his mouth and smacking his lips.

At that, Shilah turned to his brother, raising a brow. "*You* and Yaz?"

"Yep, she's been giving me cooking lessons. In exchange she allows me to give her lessons in…well, let's just say my baby is learning the ABCs of how to treat her man." A grin of remembered pleasure crossed his face. He turned to Shilah. "Just need to slice it," he said, nodding his head toward the pantry.

Holt frowned, his thumb in his mouth. "What? You don't like rye bread?"

Shilah laughed. "First you rant about her not taking care of you, then you're talking about helping her cook and then waxing poetic on how well she treats her man. ABCs of how to treat her man, my ass." Shilah laughed. "You're so whipped it ain't even funny, man."

Holt shrugged, humor lighting his pale blue eyes. "If I don't grouse every once in a while, y'all will think

I'm getting soft." He winked. "Can't have that. My babe likes me…hard."

"Whoa!" Shilah threw up his hands. "I'm a man. And your brother. That doesn't get me excited, the thought of you getting hard," he said, tossing the sack holding the bread toward Holt. Which his ex-NFL brother easily caught, an ever-present half grin on his face. "In fact, it makes me wanna hurl."

With both of his brothers, Nate and Holt, engaged, for the first time in a long time Shilah felt alone, in a way he hadn't felt in longer than he wanted to remember.

Not that he wasn't happy for them; it was just that at times lately it hit him that soon his brothers would start families of their own, and the thought was unsettling.

He lifted a bag of chips he'd found on the shelf and walked toward the island-style counter in the middle of the kitchen and placed it alongside the bread.

"You're a lucky man. Nothing wrong with appreciating what you've got."

He felt Holt's curious gaze on him as they quickly made sandwiches for their makeshift lunch.

Holt sat next to him on a barstool, took a healthy bite of his sandwich and swallowed. Around the bite, Holt began, "You know, Yaz has this friend—"

"Has Nate returned from Cheyenne yet?" Shilah interjected. There was no way in *hell* he was going to let his brother finish that particular train of thought. Damn, was he so pitiful that Holt thought he needed fixing up?

Shilah was perfectly happy remaining the single man in their family. Besides the yearning he'd felt when he'd watched his brothers with their brides-to-be, sharing secret smiles or going to bed early, eyes only for each other, Shilah knew that love and happily-ever-after wasn't in the cards for him.

He'd known that from the time he was a young boy. He was too…flawed, for any woman to ever love him.

Immediately the image of Ellie Crandall came to his mind, as unexpected as it was sudden.

He forced away the conflicting feelings he felt at seeing her again.

Although he'd chosen to go to a local college when he wasn't working at the ranch, he'd often spent his free time at the library, studying and cramming four years of college into two. Soon after graduating, he'd devoted his time fully to the ranch, working long, hard days. At that point the ranch had begun to grow—he and his brothers as well had worked alongside Jed to see to that.

Although his brothers had gone on temporarily to pursue other interests, it had been for the betterment of the ranch. Nate, the oldest, had been involved in a lucrative stint of bull riding, and Holt in the NFL. The money they'd earned was used to improve and expand the ranch.

Within a short time, their profits had skyrocketed as they'd diversified, adding breeding of thoroughbreds to their menu, the money that earned allowing them to expand even more.

It had taken the death of Jed for all three brothers to come home and work the ranch full-time, dedicating themselves to seeing it become the vision Jed had for it.

Ellie's arrival on the ranch had brought back memories, memories of a special time in his life, some painful, held deep in his subconscious, but all of them close to his heart.

"Not yet. He and Althea should be home by the weekend," Holt replied, answering his question about Nate, bringing Shilah's attention back to the present.

Recently, a national food conglomerate, Rolling Hills. had begun to buy…or consume, as he and his brothers had come to believe, many of the family-owned ranches at an alarming rate, leaving Wyoming Wilde as one of the last in the area.

Less than a year ago, a representative from Rolling Hills had approached him and his brothers in an offer to buy out the ranch. They hadn't considered the offer, although lucrative, but their refusal to sell had fallen on deaf ears.

"Any word yet on anything? Did Nate find out anything more about who, if anyone, is behind this shit?" Shilah asked, in disgust.

Not only had Rolling Hills been after their ranch relentlessly, over the last year freak accidents had been accruing at an increasing rate, from isolated fires breaking out, to animals being misplaced on their way to slaughter.

Some were minor, some more serious in nature. As the "accidents" increased, more and more the brothers suspected someone was out to get them. And the only "someone" that came to mind was Rolling Hills.

The latest incident was by far the most serious. It could prove disastrous for the ranch's continuation and was the reason Nate and Althea had made a trip to Cheyenne.

"Thank God our brother has friends in high places, or we would have been up the proverbial creek," Holt said, a hard edge entering his voice.

Nate had been tipped off by a friend who worked

for the USDA that a someone anonymous had made accusations that Wyoming Wilde Ranch was knowingly selling tainted meat.

With that, the men now knew that all the previous accidents hadn't been coincidences. Someone...more accurately, Rolling Hills, had taken the game to a whole new level, and the threat could prove fatal for Wyoming Wilde.

"I spoke with Nate this morning. Before any of this goes further, Nate's friend has arranged an outside contractor to come to the ranch and review our facilities."

Shilah frowned, thoughts of Ellie momentarily placed in the back of his mind.

"Review our facilities? What the hell for?"

Holt shook his head. "Hell, at least they didn't shut us down. Actually, it's a good thing. This way we can prove no tainted meat is coming from Wyoming Wilde." Before Shilah could comment, Holt continued. "Speaking of which," he said, standing and carrying his plate to the sink. "I don't know if you remember Doc Crandall's daughter, Ellie?" At that, Shilah's gaze flew to his brother's, narrowing.

Blithely, Holt continued, "Check this out. This could either be a good thing for the ranch or bad. Depending on how it all pans out. Anyway," he said, wiping his hands on a dishrag after cleansing the plate and placing it in the drainer, and with only a raised brow accepting Shilah's plate as well. "Turns out she followed in her old man's footsteps and became a vet."

Shilah hid his surprise at the announcement. He realized that during his earlier exchange with her he never asked Ellie what she did for a living, or what had brought her to the ranch. The thought that he might be seeing her on a more regular basis, that she might be helping her father out, filled him with a heady anticipation.

"Damn, no, I didn't know," he said, hiding his reaction.

"Gets better than that."

Shilah impatiently waited for Holt to continue, gritting his teeth when his brother frowned over the plate he'd just cleaned and *tsk*ed at himself, before wiping away a smudge of food he'd missed.

"When the hell did you become Betty Homemaker? Give me the damn plate!" Shilah said, snatching the plate and placing it in the drainer.

"Hey, what's up with you?"

Shilah exhaled a breath, knowing his behavior was odd and not wanting his brother, known for his…unusual sense of humor, to discern the reason.

"Just nerves, man. This whole thing with Rolling Hills is getting under my skin," he said, breathing a sigh of relief when his explanation seemed to appease Holt.

"Yeah, I know what you mean. Same here. Sorry about that. Guess my baby is having an influence on me when it comes to the kitchen. She pitches a fit if everything isn't cleaned up," he said with a shrug.

Although he wanted nothing more than to turn the tables and rag on Holt for his newfound domestication, Shilah's mind was divided between concern for the ranch and what, if anything, Ellie had to do with it.

He ran back through their conversation in his mind. When he'd first asked her the reason for her return to the ranch, he'd wanted to bite out his tongue, seeing the laughter flee from her eyes, replaced by the somberness that she often seemed to carry around her like a stone weight.

After that, he'd managed to bring the smile back to her face, making her laugh outright a few times, and he'd been happier than he should have been. She was just a girl from his past, he reminded himself, and immediately his inner voice mocked him with the memory of how good she'd felt…how right she'd felt against him when she'd stumbled and he'd pulled her close for a moment.

No. She was a woman from his past, one he hadn't seen or thought of for years, and nothing more.

"Yeah, well, anyway, our little Ellie has grown up and is working for the USDA. And apparently she's the vet they assigned to come and investigate."

"Wait a minute…back up. Ellie is investigating us?" When his brother stared at him as though he had grown two heads, Shilah realized that he must have lost a thread of their conversation, his mind on Ellie.

"Uh…yeah. We just talked about that. USDA is sending out their own investigator about the report?"

"Yes, I got that part. I missed the part about what Ellie has to do with that. How exactly…when….did she get involved with the case?"

"Now, that I don't know. But I'm sure Nate will fill us in when he gets back home." A glance at his watch and Holt cursed. "Damn, I was supposed to leave ten minutes ago to pick up Yaz from town."

With that he bolted out of the kitchen, leaving Shilah with his thoughts.

Left alone, Shilah thought back to his conversation with Ellie. Each time he'd been set to ask her about what she'd been doing, somehow the conversation had turned and he'd been doing the talking. A seed of doubt crept into his mind. Had she been so absorbed in him…in the conversation, to distract him away from asking what she was doing at the ranch?

He shook his head. No, not Ellie. Besides, she wouldn't do anything to harm the ranch, he reasoned. She loved it as much as any of them did.

But why hadn't she told him why she was on the ranch? The question nagged at him as he left the house, turning over in his mind Ellie's reason for not mentioning her role with the ranch.

Chapter 4

"Is that you, baby girl?"

No sooner had Ellie walked inside her parents' house, than she heard her mother calling out to her.

With a tired sigh, she placed her bag down on the hallway table and walked farther inside, spying her mother in the kitchen, an apron tied around her ample hips.

"Is Dad home?" she asked.

"No, he got a call from the Petersons. Seems one of their prize goats has gone into a difficult labor," her mother replied, casually.

Ellie laughed. To any other person that would have seemed like an odd statement, but she'd learned it all in stride, having grown up with a father who not only worked as the veterinarian for the Wilde Ranch, but also served as a veterinarian to farm animals and pets…and goat farmers. Although many of the local farms and ranches had been sold to major corporations, her father maintained a thriving practice.

She walked into the kitchen, leaned over her mother's shoulder and inhaled.

"Hmm…that smells great, Mom. What are you making?"

"Oh, just a little something I threw together."

Ellie opened the refrigerator, pulled out a can of cola and grinned at her mother.

"Something you just threw together, huh?" she asked, seeing the small smile playing around the corners of her mother's mouth.

"It's your favorite—pot roast. It's not every day my only child returns home," she quipped. Although it was said lightly, Ellie frowned. She opened her mouth to remind her mother that she didn't know how long she'd be home, but just as quickly closed it.

That was just it. She herself didn't know how long that would be.

Her return home had come at a time when she was deciding the next course in her career, her life.

Instead of joining her dad in practice after graduating, Ellie had chosen to do an extended study in animal husbandry at an overseas tertiary institution. Although her parents had been proud of her, having been chosen among thousands of applicants, she knew her father had also been disappointed that she hadn't joined him in his practice.

But, as much as she loved her parents, appreciated them, after the accident she'd suffered as a child and the looks of pity she'd come to abhor as she'd grown older,

Ellie knew that she had to leave Lander, the home she'd grown up in.

Even if that had meant leaving her parents, and the community, the only home she known for all of her life.

Completing the extended study, she'd elected to remain for a period of time as an associate professor as well as vet for the small rural community she'd come to love. But, after her last visit home, she'd been struck by how much her parents had aged despite their active lifestyle, and decided it was time to come home.

Not only for her parents, but for herself, as well.

A ghost of a smile graced Ellie's mouth as she watched her mother fussing over the food she'd prepared. Ellie had been home for almost a week, and every day her mother had "thrown together" something special for her for dinner. And breakfast, as well as anytime Ellie walked into the house.

She glanced around the immaculately kept home. Nothing was ever out of place. From the crocheted doilies set on the highly polished kitchen table that her father had made when he'd first married her mother, to the cherrywood floors and every knickknack in between, everything was neat and orderly.

Her mother turned toward her, a small smile on her face, "It's good to have you home, baby. We've missed you."

A wealth of emotion passed along the older woman's features and Ellie paused before moving toward her mother near the stove.

"Have a seat, Mom. Let me do that," she said softly. But when she tried taking the plate from her mother's hand, she was gently, but firmly, moved away.

"You go sit down and tell me how your day went. I told you…I enjoy doing this," her mother replied. Ellie shook her head, but lifted her cola can from the counter and sat at the table. Her glance went over the table set with silverware. In the middle of the table a basket was filled with bread, a large bowl of salad nearby.

"How'd the first day go? Did you get to talk to the boys?" Leandra Crandall asked, as she went about filling two plates before walking to the table and placing them down. Immediately she walked to the refrigerator and removed a pitcher of tea and brought it to the table.

Running a critical eye over the table, making sure she hadn't left anything out, finally Ellie's mother sat down next to her.

Ellie reached over to remove a roll from the basket, her stomach growling. Her mother's sharp tap on the back of her hand and scowl stopped her from taking a healthy bite. Ellie bit her lip to prevent a laugh at the silent admonishment.

"Oops, sorry, Mom," she mumbled, and bowed her head as her mother said grace.

Once her mother had blessed the food to her satisfaction, she turned to Ellie, raising a brow.

"What?" Ellie asked, swallowing down a sigh. If her mother didn't just let her eat, she would scream.

"Well?"

"Well, what?"

"Did you get to talk to the boys?" Leandra asked.

"If by boys, you mean Nate or Holt, the answer would be no."

"And what about Shilah?" her mother replied, as she began to eat.

"No," Ellie replied shortly, after a brief pause. When

her mother stared at her she felt like a deer caught in the headlights.

"What, Ma?" she asked, around a bite of food.

She felt as she had as a child whenever her parents caught her telling a lie. She felt the tips of her ears burn, something that happened whenever she hedged on the truth.

"Hmm," was her mother's noncommittal reply, and Ellie's ears burned even hotter.

After a few moments of silence, Ellie reluctantly spoke. "Okay, so I did run into Shilah. But we didn't get a chance to talk about the ranch, at least not about my involvement with the USDA."

"Oh, really? So, if you didn't talk about the ranch, what did you talk about?" her mother asked, a gleam in her eye. Ellie quickly picked up her glass of tea and took a deep drink.

"Oh, nothing important. Mainly just caught up. It's been a while since we've seen each other," she said with a shrug, forcing a lightness to her expression she was anything but feeling.

"He didn't bring up the troubles going on at the ranch?" her mother probed.

Ellie inhaled a deep breath, thoughtfully chewing. At that point she would give every one of her advanced degrees to make her mother just drop the subjects of both the Wilde Ranch and Shilah.

"No. Like I said, we just caught up on old times. Hmm, Ma, did you put cinnamon in these rolls? I really have missed your cooking," she said, smiling.

Although her enthusiastic reaction to her mother's rolls was feigned, she mentally held her breath, hoping her mother would at least take the hint that Ellie didn't want to discuss the ranch.

"Hey, thanks again for setting up my office for me, you and dad did a great job."

"Do you really like it? I didn't go overboard with all your plaques? As soon as it was official, I couldn't wait to get may hands on it and decorate," Leandra said, a smile splitting across her face. Ellie let out a long breath, relieved that she'd managed to shift the topic away from Shilah.

When she'd accepted the job offer from Jasper and Brant, a subcontractor to the USDA, along with it she was offered an office in town, set up with facilities for her to do rudimentary tests on the ranch's equipment. She'd declined, choosing instead to work out of her father's office.

Still active, her mother continued to serve as her father's assistant at his clinic. Her barely lined face belied her age, yet she, as well as Ellie's father, was in her mid-seventies.

Ellie thought back to her decision to return home, a decision she'd made well before accepting the offer to work for the USDA. She knew that, although she wasn't sure how long she'd stay here at home, she'd made the right choice.

"Do you think the boys will be okay?" her mother asked. She was pulling Ellie out of her thoughts and managing to drag the subject back to the very one Ellie was determined not to talk about.

She glanced over at her mother and saw her shifting the food around her plate with her fork, a frown marring her otherwise smooth forehead. Ellie placed her fork down and sighed.

"I'm sure they will, Mom. But you know I can't discuss the case."

She knew that her mother wanted the best for the men, for their ranch, their shared history stretching back to the days when Ellie's father and Jed Wilde had been young men. They'd both set out to accomplish goals with odds stacked against them. But Ellie couldn't discuss the case with her mother, or anyone else, outside of her direct supervisor.

Ellie didn't want to chance any sort of taint on her investigation, and the best way to do that was to keep the topic away from her involvement.

Her mother reached over and patted Ellie's hand, nodding her head in understanding.

"You don't have to say another word, baby girl. I understand. I'm sure everything will work out in the end. It always does."

"I'm sure it will, Mom."

As the two women silently finished their meal, Ellie's thoughts turned to the investigation, and she silently prayed that her mother's wish—a wish she shared—would prove true and her investigation would lead to clearing the ranch.

Chapter 5

"So, that about sums it up. With this information at least we know where we stand." Nate paused and glanced around the room. "We have an idea of what we're up against and a plan to beat it."

Althea, who stood close to Nate as he briefed the family, leaned over and grasped his hand in hers, squeezing it, giving him an intimate look. Shilah saw his brother immediately turn her way, the hard look on his face gentling, as he pulled her tighter against him before he turned back to face the family.

"The accusations aren't founded on anything more than rumor and hearsay. Good thing for us that's all they've got going right now. Whoever the hell is behind this—"

"As though we don't know who the hell *that* is," Holt broke in, disgusted, pacing the length of the living room. "We all know Rolling Hills is behind this."

Nate ran a hand through his short, thick hair and sighed. "Yeah, well, the truth is the USDA knows, as well. There was a leak within Rolling Hills that linked them with the allegations against us. None of that really matters now. USDA has no choice but to investigate all rumors—"

"Then why don't they go to the source? Stop with all the accusations against us. They know it's all bullshit, anyway—"

"Because they have to investigate, Holt. They don't… can't take accusations of mad cow lightly. It's something they have no choice but to investigate, no matter what their relationship is with us," Shilah interjected. "Look, from what you've told us it seems pretty clear what our course of action is. We sit back, participate in this investigation and let the truth speak for itself. We'll be cleared and this will be over."

It was late and everyone was starting to feel the stress from the long day. Tension was thick in the large family room where they'd gathered to discuss the additional information Nate and Althea had brought back with them.

Although the couple had returned home from Cheyenne several nights ago, this was the first time everyone had managed to get together in one place. Despite their exhaustion from the busy day, all duties had been completed or temporarily shelved in order to deal with the immediacy of their situation.

Nate had been in contact with a friend who worked for the USDA, and several months ago Nate had been told that a slaughterhouse the ranch used had been accused of selling sick cattle. Without the ranchers' knowledge, the slaughterhouse had been investigated thoroughly, but no animals, including those that came from Wilde Ranch, had shown evidence of the fatal disease.

The matter had been dropped, only to resurface last month when several children had gotten sick from meat, thought to be infected with mad cow, they'd eaten at a fast-food restaurant.

Just the mention of mad cow, particularly after a devastating outbreak that had occurred several years ago, made the USDA know it would be a public-relations nightmare if the rumor leaked to the press.

From his friend, Nate had also learned that the allegation had been lodged directly against Wilde Ranch. Although the slaughterhouse they used had been cleared earlier, because of the fear of public outcry the decision had been made to investigate the meat coming from their ranch, pending an investigation.

"Let's just be damn glad they didn't quarantine us," Shilah said, his tone grim.

"Exactly," Nate replied, his tone just as somber. "All they have is a rumor and a helluva lot of speculation—"

"A damn lie, that's what it is," Holt barked, and Nate nodded his head.

"Yeah, a lie, but a lie that could have gone a long way toward shutting us down. At least we're given the time to prove our innocence and that a lie is all this is." He paused and took a deep breath. " And that's where Ellie fits in," he said. And at mention of her name, Shilah raised his eyes, narrowed them.

"She's working as a subcontractor. She'll be at the ranch, observing the animals for usual signs of the disease, as well as taking blood samples."

"And how did she become involved?"

"This I don't know. I'm only glad that she is, not

because I expect any favors, but because she is someone we know, someone we trust. Someone we know isn't in Rolling Hills's back pocket," Nate replied.

He went on to inform them that she would be on the ranch over the next several weeks, and that she *would* have their full cooperation.

"But…despite the fact that we consider her like family, we need to keep it business. Not interfere—no taint of interference can be on this investigation. This has to be legit, up front. This is the only way to squash all the bullshit rumors."

After speaking, he glanced over at each of them, waiting for everyone's consent. When his glance landed on Shilah, he saw his brother frown, a look crossing his face, before his gaze moved on.

Shilah pushed off the wall he'd been leaning against, feeling his body tense.

"We have to clear our ranch. Our name," he finished, encompassing everyone in his statement.

Shilah's glance slid around the room, going to each face. Tension and underlying fear was thick, palpable in the room. Yet, a steely look of determination was on both of his brothers' faces, as well. The Wilde brothers wouldn't go down easily.

"I guess you're right. Ellie's investigation will not turn up one damn thing wrong with our processing of the animals, or the animals themselves," Holt said, walking over to Yasmine, looping his arm casually around her shoulders.

"I've asked her to come tomorrow and speak to the men. Explain what she's doing here, and what her role is. I've also told the men to give her their full support. Anything she asks for, any help she needs is to be given.

And of course we'll do the same," Nate finished, and everyone nodded their heads in agreement.

The birds chimed from the antique grandfather clock that stood in the corner of the room, indicating it was now past midnight.

Nate glanced toward the clock before rising, lifting Althea's hand and facing his brothers. "That's it, fam," he started. "We go on with running the ranch, doing what we do—"

"And doing it damn good," Holt interjected, a grin on his tired face.

"That's the only way we Wildes know how to do it," Shilah agreed, and the brothers all shared a look.

As they all began to disperse, Nate called out to him, asking to have a word with him before he left. Nate waited until they were alone before he began to speak.

"Shilah, we need to discuss something." Nate approached, a worried frown pulling his brows together. Something told Shilah the discussion centered around Ellie.

Although carefully keeping his expression neutral, Shilah wracked his brain wondering how…*if* his brother had somehow found out about his involvement with Ellie.

He mentally cursed. Hell, talk about jumping the damn gun. He'd only had a one-hour conversation with her and here he was thinking, if only in his mind, that they were involved.

Nate stopped in front of him, crossing his arms over his chest, and stared at Shilah. With his brows together, the expression on his set face confirmed to Shilah that somehow his brother had figured out there was something going on between him and Ellie.

Even though Shilah himself hadn't figured out exactly what that was, he was damned if he was going to allow anyone to stop him from finding out.

Shilah pushed away from the wall, feeling the muscles in his neck, his entire body, tense as he faced his brother.

"Listen, we need to talk about Ellie."

Even if that meant going against his entire family.

Chapter 6

"Was there a reason you didn't tell me you were in charge of the investigation against me and my brothers?"

Ellie jumped at hearing the deep voice and spun around to see Shilah Wilde lounging in her office doorway casually, his arms folded across his broad chest.

She clutched the file folder she held in her hand tighter, before turning back around and calmly placing it inside the drawer and closing it shut.

The sound of his voice sent a fizzle of awareness through her, unreasonable as it was sudden. Ellie drew in a deep breath to compose herself before she faced him.

"I wouldn't call it that, Shilah," she said calmly, despite the way her heart was beating out of control.

"Then what would you call it, Ellie?"

She grew uncomfortable beneath his stare. He

simply stood in the doorway, his gaze raking over her as she stood next to her desk. She sighed, blowing out a breath.

"Come in, please," she invited. After hesitating briefly, he pushed his large frame away from the doorway and moved to walk inside. "Close the door behind you, please."

She glanced toward her computer, where she'd been in the middle of shooting off an email to her supervisor at Jasper and Brant, the firm that was subcontracted with the USDA, giving him an update of her status.

She subtly pressed a button on her console, sending her computer to sleep.

"I know I should have told you the reasons I was at the ranch when we were together a few days ago. I'm sorry that I didn't." The words were inadequate, Ellie knew, and offered no real explanation.

But she had no explanation herself. All she knew was that when she'd seen him again her reasons for being at the ranch had flown from her mind.

Ellie had chosen not to examine her reasons too closely. Her encounter with Shilah, although brief, had elicited old feelings, feelings she'd had as a child, about the ranch, her accident…and Shilah.

"I wasn't trying to hide anything from you. I—I—" She stopped, sighing. "I'm sorry, Shilah."

She saw his face lose some of its stiffness, and the tension in the room eased.

"I guess it just hit me out of the blue when I was told. I wasn't expecting it. To be honest with you, it's not your fault, not really. I got so caught up in just talking to you, was so excited to see you that I didn't think to ask you myself."

The minute he finished speaking, she saw his face slightly flush, as though he hadn't meant to say what he had. She felt an answering blush on her own face.

"Anyway, I understand," he continued. "The ranch has been going through a lot…this investigation came out of nowhere for us. Had Nate not been tipped off…" When he paused this time, Ellie knew that whatever he'd been about to disclose was something she didn't need to know about.

She raised a hand. "Hey, why don't we put this out there now. I can't discuss what's going on, and neither can I know about any inner workings of the ranch."

Shilah was shaking his head before she could finish. "I know. I'm sorry. I'm sure we have other…more interesting things we can talk about."

He glanced around her office. He walked over to the wall near her desk, his gaze running over the display of her degrees and various recognition plaques, as well as a scattering of articles Ellie had written for a national vet magazine that adorned the walls.

"Dad calls that," she said, pointing to the assortment of framed certificates, "my love-me wall," she said with a small laugh.

She rose from her chair and walked toward him. "When I arrived he showed me my office and he already had it all set up. He and Mom have made duplicates of my every achievement," she said with a small shake of her head.

When she saw him smile as he reached out and fingered a framed piece of her childhood artwork, she groaned, "Even the ones dating back to kindergarten. Sometimes they go a little overboard."

He turned to face her, the familiar half smile tugging the corners of his sensual mouth up.

"They're proud of you. They have every right to be, Ellie. You're an amazing woman," he said, and Ellie flushed at the compliment.

The look in his eyes made her eyes widen. She stuck out her tongue to moisten lips gone dry. The way his eyes centered on her tongue made her flush deepen, her heartbeat banging so loudly against her chest she knew he had to hear it.

He took a step closer to her, and without conscious thought, Ellie took steps toward him, until they stood less than a foot apart. He reached a hand out to move away a strand of hair that had escaped her tight chignon, placing it behind her ear.

"You always have been," he finished, his voice low, the look in his eyes intense. As he held her gaze, Ellie searched his features, going over his strong nose, down to his sensual lips and back into his eyes. In their depths there was such a look of admiration…and something more, that Ellie turned away.

He placed a finger beneath her chin, forcing her to look up at him.

"I've missed you, Ellie Crandall," he said, his voice deep and quiet. "More than I realized."

When his head began to lower, Ellie felt her eyes begin to flutter closed.

When she felt his mouth, hard yet gentle, against the corner of her mouth, Ellie felt the tension ease from her body as the unexpected softness of his caress sent a subdued cry from her mouth.

Gently he placed a small series of kisses along

the lower rim of her mouth, undemanding, soft and inquisitive.

Ellie's hands rested on his chest, clenched, her eyes fully closed in reaction to the innocence of his kiss. Butterfly kisses turned to nibbling caresses along her lips, until with a soft moan of surrender, she eagerly rose on tiptoe to press her body closer to his.

Her action caused him to tug her closer to him, crushing her breasts against his hard chest and slanting his mouth over hers as their bodies pressed tightly together.

She inhaled a swift breath. There was nothing innocent about the feel of his shaft, hard, thick and unyielding as it pressed against her belly.

He dragged the full bottom rim of her lip into his mouth, and suckled it. Drawing lazy patterns with his tongue back and forth in the space between her lips and teeth, he wrought a deep moan from her as she arched her body fully into his chest. Slowly her hands unclenched and moved up, wrapping around his neck and drawing him closer.

His tongue moved to lave her lip and she eagerly opened her mouth wide, willingly giving him the access he was silently demanding.

When she felt his big hand, warm against her back as he lifted her sweater, running a path from up the line of her spine to the back closure of her bra, the hard ridge of his erection pressing even hotter against her stomach, warning bells rang. But Ellie chose to ignore them, too caught up in the unexpected pleasure of his mouth.

She felt him break away, and she groaned, lifting heavy eyes to look up at him.

He placed his palms against the sides of her face,

staring down at her, his breathing labored. She felt a soft tremor in the big hands that framed her face.

"God, Ellie…you taste so good. Your mouth is like honey," he told her with a catch in his voice. He bent back down to recapture her mouth, wrapping his hands around her waist, pulling her impossibly closer to his big, hard body.

Tugging her sweater away from her body, again she felt his hand against her skin, but this time he trailed a path toward her breasts. Keeping one hand on the back of her head, his lips firmly on hers, with the other hand he cupped one of her breasts. She moaned into his mouth when she felt him pinch her nipple, lightly, through the thin cotton of her bra.

Arching fully into him, her body on fire from his talented mouth, tongue and hands, Ellie tunneled her fingers through his hair, pulling him closer.

"Dr. Eleanor Crandall, you're wanted at the front!"

The sound of her father's voice, just outside her door, brought Ellie's eyes wide-open.

Dear God in heaven, what had gotten into her, she thought, panicked as she shoved Shilah away. She practically ran to the other side of the room, frantically righting her clothing.

"I—" Her father walked inside and stopped. In one glance he took in the scene, and Ellie felt her entire face flush as she placed a nervous smile on her face, glancing over at Shilah.

In the short time between her father's voice inter-rupting them and his opening the door, Shilah had swiftly straightened his clothes, yet Ellie saw the evidence of what they'd been doing on his mouth. Traces of her favorite princess-pink lipstick stained his lips.

Shilah must have realized what she was gaping at, as he casually turned away to wipe at his mouth.

Ellie walked toward her father, forcing a smile on her face. "Hey, Dad, I thought you had gone out to check on the Petersons," she said, forcing into her voice a levity she was anything but feeling.

"Uh, no, princess. I thought I'd do that after dinner. Am I interrupting anything?" he asked, turning from her and pinning Shilah with a glance.

"No, of course not. We were, uh, just going over, uh…"

Shilah walked forward and stretched out his hand. "Hi, Dr. Crandall. I happened to be in town and dropped by to ask your opinion about something," he said. "Nothing major, but since I happened to be in town, I thought I'd come by. You weren't around, and I saw Ellie here. We haven't really had the chance to catch up, so I was just in the process of trying to persuade her to go to a late lunch with me," he finished, turning to Ellie.

When her father cast a dubious glance her way, again Ellie kept the tenacious smile firmly in place, shooting Shilah a *look* from the corner of her eyes.

Josiah Crandall's glance went first to Ellie and then to Shilah, before he accepted Shilah's handshake.

"Kinda late for lunch, isn't it, baby girl?" he asked, the skepticism still in his voice.

Ellie was at a loss for words. She knew Shilah had thrown out the answer in an attempt to save the situation.

"She's been so busy here I think she forgot to eat," Shilah interjected, and again Ellie shot him an evil look.

At that, her father turned to her. "Now, I don't want

to hear your mother's mouth if she finds out I've been keeping you too busy to work! Go on, I can take over from here."

"Dad, I can't. I've got way to much work to do! I—"

Her father fixed her with a stern glance. "Go. Now."

With a sigh, Ellie lifted her hands in defeat. If for no other reason than to get her father and his scrutinizing stare out of her office, she had no choice *but* to go.

"Okay, okay, Dad…I'm going. We'll head out in a bit," she said, desperate for her father to go.

Left alone with Shilah, Ellie turned and hurried toward her desk.

"I, uh, I do have a lot of work to do, like I told my dad, so…" She allowed the sentence to dangle, as she lifted folders from her desk and restacked them in the exact same order, doing anything to keep her hands busy and face averted from Shilah.

She grabbed the stack of folders and turned to her filing cabinet, taking more time than was needed to place them in their correct file.

Dear God in heaven, what had come over her to kiss him like that? she thought, embarrassed and feeling about as sophisticated as an adolescent caught necking in her parents' house.

"Don't you think we'd better get a move on?" he asked, and she spun around to face him.

"What are you talking about?" she asked, frowning and walking back to sit down at her desk, unconsciously massaging her knee.

Her day had started off with a bang. After coming into her father's practice earlier that morning, she'd literally been on her feet the entire day. Between answering emails, assisting her father in inoculations, as well as beginning her preliminary report, it had been a hectic day for her.

Coupled with that, after leaving the clinic yesterday she'd gone out for a run, which wasn't unusual for her. She'd began running as a teenager as a form of physical therapy for her knee. Told she would regain only seventy-five percent mobility of her leg at best, Ellie had attacked her physical therapy with a vengeance.

As well as the prescribed rehab she'd undergone, she'd begun to jog, slowly at first and only a short distance, but soon she'd pushed herself and her endurance until she was able to run three miles a day at a brisk pace. Her mind heavy with her new job, she'd pushed herself further and had run until her knee had throbbed and she'd had to ice it.

Her glance stole over to Shilah. Her new job hadn't been the only thing that had been on her mind. And after the kiss they'd shared, she doubted that would change anytime soon.

"I know it's a little early for dinner, but if my guess is right, you missed lunch, right?" he asked. But before he could finish, Ellie was already shaking her head no.

"I can't. Like I told my dad, I still have a mountain of things to do before I can call it quits."

"Poor baby," he replied, and her gaze flew to his, her hand stilling on her leg. Immediately she realized she'd been massaging her knee, and she pulled her hand away, tensing.

"You do have to eat, don't you? Or do superwomen not have to?" he asked, a small smile playing around his lips.

"We do. But only on Monday, Wednesday and Fridays," she quipped back, giving him a smug look. When he laughed lightly she laughed along with him, the tension easing between them.

"I still have a lot to do, Shilah. I don't think—"

"Don't think. Just come to lunch with me. What can it hurt?" he asked, and although the request seemed casual, the look in his dark eyes as they raked over her was anything but.

Ellie felt her body react as though from a cue card. Her nipples contracted, beading against her bra, and her mouth went completely dry.

"I promise…I'll keep my hands to myself this time. You can trust me, can't you?" he asked, holding out his hand for her to take.

Her gaze slid over his tall, hard body, the jeans that molded his long legs and muscled thighs to perfection, up to his shirt which was now slightly wrinkled due to her grabbing the man as if he'd stolen something.

She stared down at his outstretched hand.

She slowly placed hers within his, all along wondering who was the one she should worry about trusting— herself or Shilah.

Chapter 7

So beautiful...

Shilah sat across from Ellie in the small booth, the lights of the pub low, lending an intimacy to the setting. His gaze raked over her face as he listened to her explain the controversy and theories surrounding the usage of synthetic hormone implants for cattle, her beautiful face animated as she spoke.

The short ride over to the pub had been mostly silent. Shilah had chosen, wisely he believed, to allow her to stay within her own thoughts, and not engage her in too much conversation. He knew part of the reason she'd accepted the invitation was to get away from her father's prying eyes.

He hoped like hell the other reason was because she wanted to be with him.

"The use of growth hormones is controversial, though

the benefits of using them are pretty impressive," she said, warming up to her topic. She stopped and shook her head, "Oh, God, here I go again, talking about something I'm sure doesn't interest you at all, Shilah."

"Ellie, there isn't anything you could say that wouldn't interest me," he replied.

"Ohh…" she said, softly, her mouth forming an O.

She bit the bottom of her lip and her lone dimple creased her cheek, tugging an answering emotion from deep inside of Shilah. For a moment they simply stared at one another until it was she who broke the connection, lifting her glass to take a small sip of her tea.

He saw the ghost of a smile cross her full lips behind the rim of the glass.

God, what she did to him with just one look, he thought, as he barely held back from releasing a groan.

Everything about her appealed to him in ways no other woman had ever been able to do for him.

From the shy smile and single dimple that would appear, the way she would duck her head slightly whenever she was embarrassed or unsure…to the way her lips felt beneath his, her slender yet curvy body molded to his as though she'd been made for him and him alone.

The thought…the memory, of the intimacy they'd shared earlier brought his shaft to half-mast. He subtly adjusted himself and took a long drink of the cold tea the waitress had placed in front of him moments ago.

"In fact, my brothers and I were recently approached last spring by a company that supplies the hormones." He said, in an attempt to get his mind…and his cock, back to safer territory.

"I'd be interested in hearing your take on it, Ellie. We've always avoided growth hormones in our cattle. Our main concern was the effect it has, long term, on the meat once it gets to the consumer."

Ellie nodded her head in agreement. "Yeah, that's the other side of the coin. While there's no argument that there are a *lot* of benefits of using growth hormones— the quality of the feed is superior...the rate of muscle development is phenomenal and the meat quality as well, *and* the fact that it provides quality meat that can be sold at more affordable prices." She stopped and shook her head. "All good arguments for their use. But you're right, there's the downside of what it can do to the consumer. Or more specifically, what we *don't* know about what it could do. The research is in its infancy stages."

"Something about using a synthetic hormones on animals that are bred for consumers..." Shilah said. "I don't know. Just doesn't seem right."

"A lot of ranchers and farmers have begun using them in their feed, more and more. I guess for their bottom line, financially, it makes sense for them."

The waitress came by to bring them their food. The minute she set the plates down in front of Ellie, the aroma hit her nostrils and her stomach growled.

Ready to continue the subject, he heard her stomach rumble, and with a shrug and a sheepish smile she took a healthy bite of her burger.

"Hmm," she said, moaning, soon after taking the bite.

"I take it it's good?" he asked, humor in his deep voice.

"Oh, my God, is it ever!"

As he watched her tongue come out to lick away the juice that had trickled down the corner of her mouth, he bit back a groan, thinking of cold showers, who would stand a chance of going to the Super Bowl, the upcoming castration planned for his steers…anything to stop himself from jumping across the table and licking the juice away himself.

"How good is it, El?" Shilah asked her, his deep sexy voice making her pause in the middle of chewing, her eyes flying to his. When she reached for the napkin he held out to her, he surprised her by moving her hand to the side and used the napkin himself to slowly wipe away the juice that had trickled down the corner of her mouth.

Her heartbeat thudded erratically, and she felt her nipples harden as though on cue, to the suggestive tone in his voice. She plastered a weak smile on her face.

"Could be that I, uh, that's it's been a long time, since I've, uh, had meat that good." She stammered out the words and immediately blushed, seeing the wicked gleam that entered into his eyes.

"Nothing like sinking your teeth into juicy, thick Wilde meat, huh?"

His words sent an illicit shiver over her body. Ellie squirmed in her seat, clenching her legs against the ache between her thighs at the image that assaulted her with his words.

He held her gaze as he lifted his own burger to his mouth. "Would you like to taste mine?" he asked, his throaty, erotic voice sending her mind and body into a heated state of hyperawareness.

"No, I, uh, I'm fine," she said, swallowing.

"Suit yourself." One side of his mouth curled and with a shrug, his strong white teeth bit into the burger. Ellie had a hard time stopping herself from reaching out and licking away the juice that slipped down over his chiseled chin, returning his earlier service to her with a twist.

The ache between her legs grew, her skin grew moist, her breathing ragged as her eyes remained riveted to his sexy mouth, and the thoughtful…careful way he chewed.

As they'd made the short drive to the restaurant, Ellie hadn't been able to think of a solid thing to say to fill in the gap of silence, her mind and body at war with her. Her mind told her going to lunch with Shilah Wilde was not only a bad choice but a stupid one at that, given her role in investigating his ranch. Her body yearned to feel him next to her again, to feel his lips against hers again, the slide of his tongue inside her mouth…

Dear God.

Ellie brought her glass of tea to her mouth with shaky hands, in an effort to both cool down the heat she felt racing over her body and to have something to do with her hands.

"The beef came from our ranch," he said, once he'd swallowed.

It took Ellie more than a few moments to gather her scattered wits. She desperately tried to untangle herself from the sensual web he'd created, one that had her heart racing as though she'd just ran a marathon.

At her frown, although the wicked gleam in his eyes remained, he explained. "The restaurants around town pretty much all use our meat. We take a lot of pride in our product." His return to casual conversation was unsettling as it was welcome.

It had been a long time, if one ever had, since a man had made Ellie feel the way Shilah had in the short time of their reunion. She wasn't sure if she felt relief or disappointment at the easing of tension, tension that stemmed from his obvious attraction to her.

She shook it off. She had no time in her life for the complication that she knew would come with Shilah. Despite their history, he was no longer the young man she'd grown up with, the one she could go to and talk about anything, the one who'd provided a safe haven for her when she'd needed it.

And she was no longer that same girl who *needed* the safe haven he'd provided, she reminded herself.

"We've worked hard for our reputation as the best. Which is another reason my brothers and I decided against using synthetic hormones." Both his tone and the expression on his handsome face grew somber. "At least until longer-term studies show there's no harm to the consumer down the line. That's more important to us, a hell of a lot more important than how much more in profits we could make, or our bottom line."

"With the way the economy has been for the last few years, the fact that you and your brothers have chosen to put the needs and welfare of the consumer first is admirable."

"When I was younger, it seemed as though we always got the scraps, meat that was days away from spoiling."

"You and your brothers? At the foster home?" she hazarded a guess.

He shook his head. "No, at the home, the state took care of most of our needs." He laughed, a humorless sound. "At least the physical ones. I meant the reservation. Even though it was a fairly large reservation, my... family, along with a few other tribe members, lived on the outskirts," he said, and she nodded.

Ellie knew that the reservation he'd lived on was fairly large, and that it brought in a lot of money from the popular casino the consolidated tribes owned. She'd mistakenly assumed that Shilah had lived there, as well.

She stored away the knowledge to think about later.

"My family, as well as the other tribe members who lived in the small community with us, got donations, for the most part, mostly from the local markets. Meat that wasn't really fit to eat." He shrugged his wide shoulders. "But, hell, beggars can't be choosy, can they?"

She reached out a hand to cover his. Shilah squeezed her hand lightly before deftly removing it, and again picked up his burger.

"Now my brothers and I supply all the beef for the subcommunity I grew up on. It was the least I...we could do," he said simply.

Ellie wanted to push for more information, wanted to find out more about this part of Shilah's life, the life he'd had before he'd come to the ranch.

She'd always known he'd grown up as a young boy on the reservation, yet despite the amount of time they'd spent together when they were younger, he'd rarely brought up that part of his life. It was something she never pushed for, yet had always wondered about.

"You have a lot to be proud of," she replied softly, deciding to allow him his privacy. When his glance met hers and she saw doubt flicker in their dark depths, she reached across the table again and took his hand in hers.

His gaze snapped to her face. "And the fact that I can call you…friend—" she stopped, swallowing down an emotion she didn't want to feel for him, much less analyze, before continuing "—means more to me than you'll ever know."

Instead of removing her hand, he brought it to his mouth, kissing the palm. She felt the dart of his tongue against her palm for a split second, his dark glittering gaze over her face, and goose bumps spiked up her arm and through her body at the sensuality of his gesture.

She inhaled a shaky breath.

Their food forgotten for the moment, it was just the two of them in the pub, and everything and everyone around faded to background noise. Ellie licked her dry mouth, heat whirling through her.

Shilah kept her hand in his, his eyes on hers as he trailed a path from her palm to her inner wrist with his tongue. He felt the shudder that ran through her, and knew she was just as affected by him as he was by her.

He saw her swallow and felt the fine tremble that shook her hand. When she tugged at her hand, reluctantly he released it.

As much as he wanted to stake a claim, he knew he had to give her room, breathing space. If only to allow her mind to catch up with what her body was telling her was the inescapable truth.

She brought her hand up and tucked errant strands that had escaped the low ponytail she wore, something he noticed she did whenever she was nervous.

"Why don't you ever wear your hair down anymore?" he asked, resisting the urge to replace her hands with his, to feel the soft, silky strands against his fingers.

She shrugged an elegant shoulder. "My hair is long and it's easier if I keep it held back, particularly when I'm seeing animals."

"I remember when we were kids, you always wore it down," he said, and laughed in memory as the image of a younger Ellie, her long brown hair flying behind her as she raced ahead of him, came to his mind.

"I've never forgotten the way you looked, racing ahead of me…"

"Taunting you because you could never beat me," she finished, joining him in the shared memory.

"Oh, I could have caught you if I'd wanted to. It was just a lot more fun letting you think *you'd* won."

At that, Ellie laughed out loud, the tension between them breaking, something he'd wanted to happen. "Oh, you could have? As competitive as you and your brothers were, even then, I highly doubt that," she scoffed. But he saw the way her eyes twinkled.

"If that helps you sleep at night, okay," Shilah replied, hiding his grin behind the rim of the glass he brought to his lips.

Her eyes narrowed. "Just admit you got beat, fair and square."

He shook his head. "Nope. Not happening. I let you win. Poor little El."

He held his breath, knowing he'd taken a gamble with that one. The jab had been intentional, meant to push past an invisible barrier he'd detected, one he'd once not felt between them.

Her eyes narrowed. "If that helps *you* sleep at night… think what you want, Shilah Wilde," she quipped, turning the tables on him. "I can take you, anytime, anyplace," she finished, reminding him of the many times she'd said the exact same thing when he'd taunted her when they were younger.

Things had just gotten a hell of a lot more interesting, Shilah thought, hiding his grin of satisfaction.

Chapter 8

"We've got ten pens set up and the men have rounded up roughly 70 to 75 cattle to start. That sound about right? Is that the number you were thinking to start with, El?"

Ellie turned around and glanced over her shoulder at Shilah as he sat astride his large stallion, his gaze fixed on the pen holding the cattle in preparation for the first stages of Ellie's investigation.

Ellie frowned, running a critical glance over the large pen. "Hmm," she murmured, biting the corner of her lip, her brow furrowed in concentration. She checked the small clipboard she held, containing notes that she used religiously whenever doing fieldwork. She took pride in the detailed system she'd created on paper, hoping it would work the way she'd planned; she hoped it would create a viable way to maximize results and keep chaos minimal.

As had been the plan, Ellie had taken the time the previous week, before actually coming to the ranch to work out the system she'd designed, to not only create her methodology, but to also set up her lab at her father's clinic.

Although the blood she'd be drawing from the cattle would be sent to the lab in Cheyenne, Ellie also planned to review it, as well.

Although she knew…prayed, that the evidence would prove the men's animals were free of disease, she wanted the reassurance that she had done everything in her power to keep the research pure.

That was the part of the process she enjoyed the most—research. In school it was what she'd excelled at, and was one of the reasons she'd won out for the scholarship to learn abroad. It was also what had eventually led to her being asked to take on this case.

The only thing that put a damper on her enjoyment of this particular research was the reason she had to do it, and for whom. The risks and consequences for the ranch, if she were to find out there was indeed evidence of mad cow disease, would be catastrophic.

"You know, I think this is just about the right amount we need for now, Shilah," she answered, raising her voice so he could hear her over the loud cries of the cattle.

"Great, so what's the objective for today? I just want to make sure I'm clear so I can relay the information to the men. Don't want to take any chances on this not being done right. A lot is riding on this," he said in his deep voice, sending a fizzle of heat over Ellie, a reaction she ruthlessly forced to the side.

There was no room for that. She was on the ranch for

one reason, and one reason only—to do the job she was paid to do. Without fail she would do that job without interference from anyone, least of all Shilah Wilde.

She glanced back over at Shilah. Despite the smile on his face, there was a hint of grimness in his tone. Ellie completely understood the reason for the strain, which mimicked the tension she herself was feeling.

As he was looking over the cattle, a slight frown marring his perfect face, Ellie in turn allowed herself to look at him fully, drawing in a deep breath of resignation.

He wasn't supposed to be here with her. When she'd met with Nate yesterday and they'd gone over the tentative plans for the next two weeks, she'd been assured neither he nor his brothers would be here while she conducted the research.

Instead, he'd informed her that she would be working with Jake, who was the ranch's foreman, along with a crew Jake was already in the process of assembling to assist her in any way she needed.

Nate had told her in no uncertain terms that neither he nor his brothers wanted be involved. They all knew the seriousness of the situation, and didn't want there to be any question of bias, based on Ellie's history as a family friend, or her father as the ranch's vet. Nate had gone on to tell her that they felt confident their animals were clean and the investigation was one that had their full backing, knowing it would exonerate the ranch in the end.

Nate's heartfelt assurance had gone a long way in easing the last of the discomfort she'd felt in accepting the position, as had the brief hug he'd given her, welcoming her back home.

Surprised at the unexpected display of friendship, a friendship that dated back to childhood, she'd blinked several times, battling back the emotion she felt from the small, but sincere, gesture.

She'd had mixed feelings about accepting the position, one that had been extended to her after her involvement in a similar investigation, two years ago.

Having worked with the USDA as a subcontractor before, Ellie's name was in the database and, as only a select number of veterinarians in the country had her particular expertise, she'd been offered the position.

However, when offered the position, Ellie had given her supervisor full disclosure regarding her association with the ranch. After a careful review of her records, she'd been approved.

She knew that was partly due to the fact that her supervisor had not only worked with her during the previous assignment, but that he'd once taught a class she'd attended. He assured her he believed her ethics were beyond reproach and her familiarity with the Wildes wouldn't interfere with her performing her job.

Although she'd discussed it with her father before accepting the position, it had taken Nate's warm acceptance of her as well as the job she was there to conduct before Ellie felt at ease.

Additionally Nate had assured her that neither he or his brothers would interfere with the investigation, and would give her the space she needed to work without them hovering.

His reasons had mimicked the very same reasons she'd given Shilah when he'd taken her to lunch.

At the time when he'd told her, she knew she *should* feel pleased. Yet she found herself wondering if the decision had been a unanimous one between all the brothers. Particularly Shilah.

She turned back around and found Shilah's dark gaze focused intently on her and suppressed a shiver.

So much for giving her the "space" Nate had promised.

As much as she knew he shouldn't be there with her, having given her objections when he showed up that morning soon after her arrival on the ranch, there was no use lying to herself like she wasn't glad he was there.

Expecting to be with the foreman, as had been the plan, Ellie arrived in time to see Nate and Shilah involved in a…discussion. The argument had been short and to the point, and although she'd only caught the tail end of it, and had been too far away to really hear the conversation, Ellie could feel the anger rolling off both their big shoulders as the two men faced off.

Ellie wondered at Shilah's reasons for going against Nate's wishes. A part of her hoped it wasn't just to keep an eye on her, but because he hadn't been able to get her out of his mind, as she hadn't been able to keep her thoughts away from him.

"Ellie? The men are ready to roll. Which pen do we tackle first?"

With a start, Ellie turned to see Shilah staring across at her. She knew there was no way he could know the direction of her thoughts, but there was something about the way he was looking at her, in that certain way he alone had, even when they were younger. It made her feel as though he could read every single thought in her mind, that he could somehow see deep inside, to the very heart of her.

A ghost of a smile played around his mouth, making her heartbeat speed up just the smallest bit, and a bead of sweat trickled down between her breasts, despite the way the day had cooled. Her nipples responded on cue to his stare.

She felt them constrict painfully, as though he'd touched them. As though they were reaching out to him for his touch.

She brought herself up short when she consciously found her body leaning toward him, his horse inches from hers.

She drew in a shuddering breath and turned, breaking the visual connection.

Dear God, she was losing it. Ellie shook her head as though to clear it, desperately trying to call up what her response was supposed to be, mentally scrambling to remember what his question had been.

A frown marred his perfect features. "Are you okay, El?" he asked, his voice deep with worry.

"I—I'm fine," she said. Removing her hat, she ran her hand through her hair, dampened with sweat. "Just tired, I guess," she said, although that had nothing to do with the reason for her momentary memory loss.

His glance fell from her face, down the line of her neck, and stopped at the valley of her breasts. As though he knew what was happening to her.

As though he knew he was the cause.

Ellie's body tightened. It was as though he'd touched her, as though she could feel his strong hands brushing over her breasts.

"How about we go with the red team?" he asked, referring to the red bar code she'd placed on one of the pens.

"Yes…that sounds good," she said, keeping her thoughts firmly under control. "We'll color-code the cattle according to the pen they'll go in. Tell the men to herd them in, ten at a time, so as not to scare them."

While in veterinary school, Ellie had learned of a technique that seemed very effective for keeping cattle calm, a state she wanted them to be in. She would not only be drawing blood from them, but also observing them for physical signs of stress and other ailments to make her full assessment.

"Sounds great, doc," he quipped. "You're the boss," he said with a wink, a sexy smile crossing his sensual mouth, and Ellie was helpless against the humor and the smile.

"And don't you forget it," she replied, keeping her face stern, refusing to respond to either the humor or the way his smile made her insides go to pure jelly.

"Not likely to forget."

"Then we can take the next shipment and place them in the pen adjoining, and we'll start tagging the remaining," she went on, fighting to keep the conversation on business.

"Hmm." She stopped, thinking momentarily. "I'm thinking the quickest way, probably the most efficient way, would be to tag them after they've had the first blood drawn. We then keep those cattle in the same pen together, for observation. This will eliminate crowding and keep them calm. After they've been cleared the men can release them. I'll have their blood stored and we'll move on to the next group. That's pretty clear, right?" Ellie asked, scrunching her nose, running her gaze over the open area filled with the waiting cattle.

The task wasn't an easy one, but she knew it was manageable as long as everyone was on the same page.

"Clear as mud!" was his reply. Startled, Ellie glanced away from the cattle and laughed lightly. Although she'd been asking the question of him, actually she'd been voicing out loud her thoughts, something she often did.

"Great, as long as we're clear…at least I'm assuming being clear as mud is a good thing?" she asked, and he laughed along with her.

"Yep. Pretty sure I've got it straight," he said with a wink.

"I'll get the men right on it. Shouldn't take us more than a few of hours to get through the first pen, draw the blood and tag the cattle. The men I've chosen for this job are pretty experienced with this," he said. He turned, reining in his horse, and galloped toward the holding pen where the men were beginning the systematic separation of the cattle.

Maybe she'd conjured up in her mind that what she'd seen in his eyes, the look of admiration and longing, had been nothing more than leftover sentiments from days gone by.

But on the heels of that thought surfaced memories of their kiss, the way he'd held her. Mentally throwing up her hands, Ellie threw herself into work.

She began the arduous task of cataloguing the cattle, the first step in her process before she'd draw blood and perform her observations. Ellie wasn't even aware of the passage of time, her day flying by.

Ellie rubbed at her knee, feeling tension form a tight knot beneath the surface.

Throughout the day, she'd alternated between riding horseback, helping to herd the cattle into their assigned pens, and drawing blood from the cattle, labeling the vials and then observing the animals for signs of illness.

Many times she'd felt Shilah's eyes on her, and it was those times she'd taken pains not to rub at her knee, not wanting him to know how badly it was beginning to ache.

He must have seen her, because toward the end of the day, when they had two pens of cattle left to get through, he called for backup.

No sooner had he called out for his men to round up more help, than Ellie was shaking her head, giving a counterorder.

A young ranch hand glanced from Ellie's set features to Shilah's, the boy's face bewildered, not sure who he should listen to.

Ellie sighed and turned to Shilah, knowing the young man was waiting for his boss to give him the final verdict.

"I thought we agreed...out here, I'm the boss," she said, and held her breath, seeing indecision cross his face.

He stared over at her, and despite the set expression, she saw the underlying look of concern reflected in his eyes as his glance slid over hers.

"We can pick this up tomorrow, El," he said, his voice low, for her ears alone.

"I'm fine," she replied, yet was touched by his concern. Their horses were so close that they were almost touching noses. Impulsively, Ellie reached across the short expanse between them to place a hand over his large forearm. As soon as her hand touched his, she felt the thick muscle bunch beneath her fingertips.

He held her gaze, lifted her hand from his arm and brought it to his mouth, where he placed a soft kiss in the center of her palm. Ellie felt the light caress sear a path straight from her palm throughout her body.

"Shilah—" she choked out.

"I know you're in pain, Ellie," he interrupted, quietly, for her ears alone.

She felt none of the shame and anger she normally felt whenever she detected sympathy from those around her. It was somehow…different, the sympathy she felt from Shilah. A connectedness that went beyond the physical, one that left her shaken.

As though everyone around them had disappeared, the noise from the cattle and ranchers yelling out orders all faded to nothingness and there was only her and Shilah, alone.

"Shilah…I'm fine," she whispered and, after a long appraisal of her, he nodded his head shortly.

"Fine. But we're calling it quits after this last bunch." When she opened her mouth to argue he cut her a look.

Ellie held up both hands in surrender. "Okay, okay… but tomorrow we'll be on an even tighter schedule. Hope you can handle it," she quipped, but was secretly glad that he'd taken the decision out of her hands.

"Oh, don't worry about that," he said, running a long, hot glance over her. "There's not much I can't handle, doc…. You'll do well to remember that," he said. Without waiting for her reply, he tugged on the horse's reins and galloped away, leaving Ellie's mouth open as she stared after him, wondering what the hell to make out of *that*.

Chapter 9

Ellie leaned back in her saddle, closed her eyes and allowed the cool air to blow across her hot skin, fighting back the disappointment she felt.

The day had been long, hard and dirty. With a sigh, she removed her hat, running a hand through her sweat-dampened hair.

They'd finished for the day, and the men had left, along with Shilah. After the day spent with him, working side by side, she expected...

"What exactly were you expecting?" she asked herself, aloud, in the dark.

She didn't expect what had happened—for him to leave along with the men and barely say goodbye to her.

After they'd left, she'd been torn. Although she was so tired she could barely move, she was also strangely restless. Not quite sure what to do with herself, Ellie had decided to go for a ride and had resaddled her horse.

Since her arrival, she'd yet to take a ride, remembering how it used to calm her, the feel of the wind blowing against her face, the natural sounds of the night, birds cawing, crickets chirping, mixed in with the occasional horse neighing and calf moaning, all blended together to make what Ellie like to think of as…

"Ranch music," a deep voice filled in the thought.

With a start, Ellie's eyes flew open and she turned to see that Shilah had ridden up next to her. Lost in her thoughts, she hadn't heard him.

"What?" she asked, turning toward him, telling herself that the reason her heart had jumped was because he'd scared her, and not because she was happy to see him.

He smiled across at her. "Remember, you used to call it ranch music?" he asked, and the frown on her face eased, softening into a smile and she laughed softly.

Ellie shook her head. "I can't believe you remember that." She paused for a moment, and plunged in, asking, "Wanna go for a ride?"

"Thought you'd never ask," he said with a slow grin.

Ellie reined in her horse, coming to a stop, completely out of breath.

They'd ridden for the last hour, and although she could have ridden another hour, she knew if she did, her body would be screaming at her in the morning from the aches and pains.

As she was turning to face Shilah, who'd slowed his horse down as well, she stopped, squinting.

"Is that what I think it is? It's still there?" she asked, pointing. In the distance stood a lone old cabin, one she and Shilah used to play in, from the time they were children until she'd left the ranch.

He smiled at her. "It is…. Wanna check it out?"

Ellie hesitated, glancing down at her watch, the illuminated dial indicating the lateness of the hour.

"No, I better not. It's getting late," she said, her tone wistful.

"Come on, El…I'll race you there," he threw out the challenge. That was all she needed.

Pulling on the reins of her horse she nudged it, leaned down low, urging her horse to go, her laughter trailing behind her as she took advantage of Shilah's surprise and got a head start.

She made it to the cabin moments before he pulled in next to her, both of them completely out of breath.

He raised a brow at her, taking in deep, even breaths. "You cheated."

"All's fair in love and war," she replied, completely unrepentant of her unfair advantage. "Come on," she said. Before she could dismount, he was there beside her, holding out his hand for her to take.

Together they walked up the short walk, until they reached the cabin, the old floorboards creaking beneath their booted feet.

"Hey, be careful," Shilah murmured, cupping her beneath the elbow. "Here, let me help you." She allowed him to help her navigate the rickety stairs, until they reached the door.

"You think it's unlocked?" she asked, biting her bottom lip and glancing up at him in question.

"Only one way to find out," he said and leaned out, grasping the rusted doorknob.

When the door opened easily, Ellie gave Shilah a surprised look.

He grinned, motioning for her to go in front of him. "After you."

Once inside, Ellie turned by instinct, memory flooding her of the layout of the place, and found a light switch. When the light flickered on, she smiled in surprise.

"Not only is it open, but it still has electricity," she marveled, glancing around at the small cottage. As she did, memories of days gone by flashed in her mind.

"No, we never had the electricity turned off," Shilah replied, following her as she walked through the small living room, running a hand over the back of the single sofa in the center.

A scarred coffee table was set in front of it, and in the corner stood a bookshelf still holding books.

Ellie turned to face him, a frown and a look of question on her face. "Shilah…it's as though we never left! I mean, everything is exactly like I remember it," she said. Without giving him a chance to comment, she continued to walk through the small cabin, her amazement growing as she spun around to face him.

"Shilah?" she asked, confusion turning to dawning realization when she saw what looked like a blush darken his olive-colored face.

"Shilah…did you keep it like this?"

He avoided her glance, and she walked over to him, placing a hand on his arm. "Why?"

"Come on, El…you know why."

Ellie felt as though all the air had been sucked from the room as his dark gaze settled over hers. Confused, not wanting to try and figure out what it all meant, she turned away.

"I—I think we'd better go."

"What are you so afraid of, El?" he said, pulling her around to face him, his face tightening with anger.

When Ellie tried to shrug off his hold on her, he placed two fingers on the side of her chin, forcing her to hold his gaze. "What about me scares you?" he demanded.

She placed her hands on his chest and shoved him away, suddenly angry. Angry at the situation, the way he made her feel…at herself for not being able to turn away from the dark promise in his eyes.

"Afraid of you?" she scoffed, rolling her eyes. "I'm not afraid of you or anyone else. Whatever misconceptions you have in that head of yours about me, you can just forget. I. Am. Not…afraid of you," she reiterated, dragging each work out, staring at him defiantly. She ignored the inner taunting voice that asked who she was trying to convince, Shilah or herself.

The anger left his eyes, replaced with a look that made Ellie draw in a breath, her eyes widening at the intense way he was staring at her.

His unflinching gaze trained on her, his focus shifting from her eyes, down to her mouth, and back. She felt herself go still beneath his perusal.

It was as though he was trying to look into her very soul.

Ellie felt chill bumps feather along her spine, down her body, and trembled.

It was as though he sought to discern her every thought, push past every barrier she'd ever erected, barriers she'd worked her entire life to build.

In that moment, it was as though all the layers of her life came tumbling down. Her breath grew ragged, her chest heaved as she fought a battle she could not see, one that she'd been waging against the world in an effort to keep herself, her emotions, her very self at a distance.

She pushed against the stonelike wall of his chest to no avail. Angry tears rimmed her eyes, but she stubbornly fought against them, determined to hold them at bay.

"What—" She stopped, breathed in deeply before continuing. "What do you *want* from me, Shilah?"

For long moments he didn't speak, so long she wondered if he'd heard her whispered plea, or if he had, whether he would answer her.

She felt his finger beneath her chin, forcing her to raise her eyes to meet his.

The heated look in his eyes as he stared down at her sent a curl of desire through her body. A deep emotion filled his dark eyes' depths, so much emotion she turned her head away, unable to believe…accept what she saw.

She felt his lips touch the top of her head in a soft caress.

"It's just you and me, Ellie. Just like it always has been. You don't have to hide from me."

He ran his finger down the side of her face. Before she realized what she was doing, Ellie turned into his hand, rubbing her head softly back and forth against his palm.

He turned her face so that she was forced to look at him, and she saw a small smile lift the corner of his sensual mouth. Although he smiled, there was no humor in his dark gaze, only simmering desire and something more…intangible, fleeting, so fleeting that she thought she'd imagined it.

He leaned down and tilted her face to meet his mouth. He simply brushed his lips back and forth over hers in feathery strokes, before slowly lifting his head.

"I can't do this, Shilah. I—" She turned away from him, turned away from the smoldering look in his eyes, away from what his eyes were telling her he wanted from her.

Afraid to see her own need mirrored within his hot gaze.

"You don't have to *do* anything, Ellie."

As she began to pull away he grasped the side of her face and placed another kiss on her lips.

Ellie released a shuddering breath.

"Just feel."

This time when he lowered his head, he did so slowly, as though giving her time to move away, if that was what she wanted. To give her time to deny him…herself, the truth of what was brewing between them. A truth that stretched back years, a connection that went deep and one that left Ellie feeling shaken and afraid.

Ellie stared up at him, meeting his gaze, unable to move away.

His minty breath brushed the side of her face, the end of his nose nudged her cheek in a soft back-and-forth motion.

"The only other thing I want from you is to tell me you want me, Ellie," he whispered, against the corner of her lips.

Ellie moaned, softly, trapped in the sensual web he'd created; one she had willingly allowed to capture her. "Tell me this isn't one-sided."

She felt his hands tunnel through her hair, dislodging the band that held it back. Sifting his fingers through her strands, he tugged her close and slanted his mouth over hers.

In feathery strokes he ran his mouth over hers in easy glides, back and forth, his tongue sneaking out to lick across the seam of her lips.

The touch of his tongue was electric fire and as Ellie gasped, her mouth opened to allow him entry.

As soon as she opened her mouth to him, his hungry tongue invaded, swirling around the moist cavern of her mouth, running along the length of her teeth, end to end, before diving deep to leisurely lap and toy with her tongue, in a heated love play that wrung a deep moan from Ellie.

"Tell me that you want me as badly as I want you," he said, his breathing heavy as he broke away from her.

"I—I—" She stopped, unable to voice what she felt in her heart. Confused, tears burned the back of her eyes. She couldn't put into words something she hadn't given a name to herself. With a cry, she turned away.

But, he wouldn't allow her even that.

He pulled her tighter, closer, until her breasts pressed hotly against the hard wall of his thick chest. His hands came out to cup her cheeks, brushing away the tears she hadn't known she'd shed.

Her hands came out to cover his, trembling.

She stared up at him with desperate eyes. "I—I don't know what's wrong with me." The admission was torn from her, as emotions crowded in on her. "I just can't do this, Shilah, I just can't."

"Let me take care of you, Ellie. No questions, no examination of what this is between us." The ends of his nostrils flared, his gaze going over her, as his hands trailed down from her face, down the side of her neck and over her body, deftly removing the jacket she wore, allowing it to fall on the floor beside them.

"No expectations, no recriminations."

His fingers delved back into the back of her head, pulling her head closer while the other hand moved down her body, past the swell of her hips, and palmed her buttocks.

She drew her bottom lip into her mouth, her heart pounding when so close to him, their bodies pressed together, she could feel every long hard inch of his arousal as it pressed into her belly.

Her nipples spiked and she arched her back, as his hands slid up and beneath her sweater, his cool palms sliding against her overheated skin.

He slanted her head, and brought their mouths together, his tongue immediately invading her mouth again. He tugged at the lower rim of her mouth with his teeth and suckled it until she hissed in pleasure.

Of their own volition her arms crept up and snaked around his shoulders, tugging him down even closer to her.

Her body on fire for him, she mewled, rubbing her body against his, silently begging for him to continue his sensual assault.

One big hand reached for her breast, running his fingers over the silky material, thumbing at her nipple, pinching and toying with it until it pearled beneath his talented fingers.

Long, drugging kisses later, he wrenched his mouth from hers, his nostrils flaring, chest heaving with each harsh breath he took. When he withdrew from her, her eyes flew open, a soundless cry of denial on her lips.

When Shilah broke their kiss, his breathing harsh, he stared down at her, his hands trailing over her nearly naked torso, until they came to rest at her breasts.

Although slender, her breasts were round, high and firm. He trailed his fingers over them, lifting them, cupping them in the palm of his hand.

Her sexy, lacy red bra was striking against her deep chocolate skin, the lace barely covering the slight swell of her breasts.

So damn sexy…just looking at them made his mouth water and his shaft thump against the constriction of his jeans.

He wanted…needed to see them. Feel them in his mouth…taste and caress them. The thought brought his erection to painful proportions.

He quickly unfastened the front closure of her bra and watched in hot fascination as her breasts bounced free. Her nipples, long and erect, looked like tight little cherries perched on top of a dark, decadent piece of chocolate cake.

He grabbed her, lifting her and, straddling her legs around his waist, he turned.

"Shilah, what—" she began, and he slanted his mouth over hers and walked the few steps toward the kitchen table, and placed her down on it. Before she could ask anything further, with a groan he leaned down and captured one of the cherry-colored nubbins with his teeth.

He heard Ellie's moan, and the feel of her hand on his head, as she tugged his head closer. He bit down on her nipple, not hard enough to hurt, but enough so that he knew she felt the sting.

She moaned and clutched at his head, dragging him closer as she arched her breast fully into his mouth.

Shilah glanced up at her through a haze of lust and sweat, watching her, her head thrown back, her fingers digging into his scalp, as he licked her breasts, alternating his attention from one to the other, before suckling one deep inside his mouth. Back and forth he laved her, greedy for her, her taste driving him out of his mind. The sight of her obvious pleasure enflamed him even more.

Without a word, he dropped down on his knees in front of her. He had to taste…more of her.

He kept his eyes fixed on hers as his fingers went to the fastening of her jeans, unbuttoning one, two, a third before Ellie came out of her sensual daze.

"Shilah…no…" she whispered, staring down at him, pushing away the greedy anticipation she felt after reading the clarity of his intent in his dark eyes.

"Let me do this, Ellie. Just for you."

Ellie swallowed deep, her heartbeat thudding an erratic pattern against her chest. Her eyes fluttered closed when she felt the brush of his big hand over the silk of her panties.

She held her breath, expelling it in one long whoosh of air when she felt his finger pull at the side of her panties and one big finger ease inside.

When he eased a second finger inside, and grasped her clit, rolling it between his thumb and forefinger, her moans increased, the sound of her cries echoing in the room as he took her own moisture and, separating her vaginal lips, spread it between her moist folds before slowly, God, so slowly, easing a finger inside her clenching heat.

When she felt his tongue lightly stroke across her mound, her eyes flew open and she stared at the top of his dark head, between her thighs.

"No, Shilah...*nooo*." Her denial ended in a long cry, as he ignored her pleas, ministering to her body as though he had every right.

In a slow, easy rhythm he paid homage to her body, licking and stroking her in languid turns, dragging his finger in and out of her core, while his talented, wicked tongue made almost lazy swipes between her drenched folds. He played and toyed with her until her body was at a fever pitch.

Every muscle tensed and she reared her body up, grabbing his head and helplessly moving her body against his.

Ignoring her pleas, he continued to minister to her, easing his finger in and out of her, his rhythm slow and easy, as he took his time with her, toying with her, until she could take no more.

"Shilah!" she screamed as she felt the beginnings of an orgasm unfurl. Her body strummed with pleasure, electrified and on fire...it no longer belonged to her. It belonged to Shilah.

She moaned, moving against his finger, as his nimble fingers and lips were busy catering to her in ways no man had ever done to her before, gifting her with a pleasure she'd never felt.

"Ohhhhh," she panted, her breath coming out in painful gasps.

"So good," he murmured, kissing her nubbin, drawing

it deeply into his mouth and slowly allowing it to pop out. "So, sweet," he mouthed the hot words against her pulsing core.

"Oh, Shilah…" The words were a long hiss of pleasure from Ellie's partially open mouth.

The ache between her legs grew tauter, and her heart felt ready to explode from her chest when she felt his big hand press above her mound, at the same time his tongue captured her straining bud and tugged, hard.

With her eyes tightly clenched, a kaleidoscope of color bursting behind them, she gave in to the mind-blowing orgasm. With feverish abandon she rode the crest of the orgasm, barely feeling the tight hold he now had on her legs as he grasped her hips, his mouth nestled between her thighs as he continued his sensual assault.

When the last shuddering contraction left her body, she weakly fell back against the table, her body spent.

Ellie felt him move up her body, felt the tug of her jeans as he closed and fastened them for her, but unable to move, much less assist him, she lay on the table, eyes closed as reality came crashing down on her.

He rose to his feet, and she felt him near her. Unable to open her eyes and face him…what she'd allowed him to do, she turned her face away. Emotions crowded in on her so tight she felt as though they were choking her, sucking out the very air around her.

She felt his hands beneath her body and tensed. Lifting her in his arms, he turned and sat down with her, cradling her in his lap.

"Shilah," she began to speak, her voice raspy.

He placed a finger over her lips. "It's okay, baby."

He laid his cheek on top of her head and Ellie felt tears burn her eyes.

As though he knew the emotions she felt crowding in on her were too much for her to handle.

She also knew that she wasn't alone in how she felt.

With her ear pressed against his chest, she heard the pounding of his heart, felt the hard ridge of his erection against her bottom, but he made no demands on her.

His kisses, the unselfish way he'd loved her…and now the amazing selfless way he held her, with no demand, made her feel more desired…beyond the physical, than she ever had in her life.

Later, later she'd think about the ramifications of what she'd allowed to happen. For now, she simply lay against him, cherishing the feel of his chest, and the feel of his body close to hers as her eyes slowly drifted down and she fell asleep.

Chapter 10

Ellie returned home to an empty house. Walking into the kitchen, she found a plate of food, covered, waiting for her on top of the stove.

Next to the plate was a note from her mother, telling her not to wait up for them as they'd decided to go to dinner and a late-night movie with friends.

"Thank heavens for small favors," she muttered, grateful to have the house to herself, if only for a few hours. She needed to decompress without having to put on a facade of nonchalance in front of her parents. Wearily she made her way toward her bedroom.

Not that she would have been all that successful if she'd had to. The type of acting that would require was way above her abilities, and her very discerning parents would have seen right though her.

Running strictly on autopilot, after taking a brisk

shower she rummaged through her chest, hunting out her favorite comfort clothes—flannel lounging pajamas, thermal shirt and the pièce de résistance…thick cotton panties, or what she liked to call her favorite granny panties.

Before leaving her bedroom she pulled a pair of equally ugly but no less comforting granny socks on her feet to complete the outfit.

Comfort clothes. Just what the doctor ordered.

After dressing she made her way back downstairs and headed toward the living room. Her stomach growled, reminding her of the food her mother had left.

After heating the dish, she lifted the lid and the aromatic smell of the seasoned pot roast and garlic potatoes brought a blissful smile to her face.

It was as though her mother knew she needed the familiarity of her favorite food.

Just like the clothes, the food would serve as the perfect comfort and maybe force the image from her mind of Shilah's dark head buried between her legs as he'd catered to her in the most intimate way.

"Fat chance that's gonna happen," she said with a humorless laugh. She was just thankful she hadn't had a wreck on the way home, her mind not on the drive but what they'd done…what she had *allowed* to happen, occupying her thoughts instead.

With a self-directed growl of frustration, she ruthlessly shoved the heated memories to the side.

Grabbing a cola from the refrigerator, she placed it along with the plate of food on a tray and walked over to the living room.

She blew out a long breath and lay back against the back of the sofa. Lifting the fork to her mouth, she took a bite of food before reaching for the remote and channel searching, looking for anything that would keep her mind busy, active and away from Shilah.

She gave up after going through every one of the 200-plus shows, wondering how there could be so many choices and nothing to see.

With a sigh, she gave up, tossed the remote on the table and lifted the fork, only to move it around the plate, before putting it, and the plate back down on the table.

As much as she enjoyed her mother's cooking, tonight even that didn't seem to give her the comfort she was looking for. She suspected nothing was going to do that for her.

With a heavy sigh, she lay back against the sofa, mindlessly watching *Judge Judy*. Even that didn't seem to give her the comfort she was looking for.

More than the memory, which seemed to be seared in her brain for all time, were the potential ramifications that could result from what she'd done. As her father was fond of saying, shit could seriously hit the fan after this.

She settled farther back into the cushions of the sofa, sighing.

She was going to have to face what she'd done, and move on. That was all there was to it. She could handle it. She was a successful, mature adult. A woman who knew her own mind, and one who didn't allow her emotions to rule her better judgment.

Tomorrow she'd face Shilah and explain to him, rationally, that what happened could...*would,* never happen again. She was there for one reason and one reason only, and that was to complete her investigation, and she wouldn't allow anything to get in her way of doing that.

Even if that something came in the form of six feet three inches of smoldering masculinity with enough crazy hot sexuality to make a nun reconsider her vows.

"Oh, shut up," she mumbled aloud to her mocking inner voice that promised it would take a heck of a lot more than a few Hail Marys for her to accomplish that goal.

Shilah lay alone in bed, staring up at the skylight in his ceiling, thinking of what had happened between him and Ellie with his shaft still semi-erect. A state that seemed to be a regular for him, since Ellie had re-entered his life.

Making love to her wasn't something he'd planned, but neither was his life turning upside down and inside out the way it had since her return.

With a low growl he turned back on his side, as even the damn skylight reminded him of Ellie.

He'd had the skylight built into his ceiling when they'd begun the renovations on the house, several years ago. All because of an off comment Ellie had made when they were teenagers.

It had been the end of spring, and an unusually warm day. They'd been outside, lying on the grass staring up at the moonlit sky. Ellie had driven up with her father as he'd been inoculating the animals and, when Shilah had asked her to stay longer, she'd given him a shy smile and gotten permission from her father.

That night stood out for him for two reasons. One reason was that it had been the last time the two of them were alone together.

Secondly, because it was then that Shilah realized that he cared about her in a way that went beyond mere friendship. But he'd never told her.

Now as he lay in bed he wondered if fate had intervened and given him a second chance with her. If he could find out whether the feelings he had were strong, real, and if she felt anything for him, a small glimmer of the wild way he felt about her.

Or, if as before he'd allow the fear of rejection, a rejection that seemed to follow him around like some sort of wounded dog, would again prevent him from telling her how he felt.

He laughed humorlessly, thinking how he'd pushed thoughts of her aside all these years, afraid to examine his feelings for her.

Restless, he turned over in bed again, punching the pillow into shape.

The semi-erect state became a full-blown hard-on as his mind filled with images of her beautiful body, partially exposed to him, the feel of her perfect breasts filling his mouth…the taste, the fragrance of her femininity still in his nose…his breath.

He inhaled a low, shaky breath.

The erotic images, coupled with the state of his arousal, promised for a long, *long,* restless night.

Chapter 11

"I'll take the rest of these to the men, Ms. Lilly," the young girl said, lifting the heavy basket in her thin arms.

"Anna, you can't do that alone! I'll get one of the men to help you," Lilly said with a frown. She watched the girl lift the basket filled with food to take to the canteen.

"Yaz, baby, go on and get Holt. Tell him we need help…. I know that boy ain't too far away. Unless he's working, he's usually within yelling distance from you." Lilly turned to Yasmine, who was in the process of pulling a tray filled with an assortment of goodies from the oven. "I swear, the way you two act around each other, it's a wonder either one of you ever gets any work done."

"Uhh…kinda busy with this, Aunt Lilly," Yasmine said, as she placed the cooking pan on top of the large double oven.

"Ohh, that smells delicious…gimme gimme gimme," Althea said from across the kitchen without looking up.

"None for you!" Yasmine said in her best "Soup Nazi" imitation from a long-running sitcom.

"No, really, I can handle it," Anna said, and before Lilly could stop her, with only a slight stumble to her walk, she rushed from the kitchen.

"Yaz, you don't want to mess with a woman on the verge of a breakdown!"

"Breakdown from what?"

Lilly spread her hands over the food-filled basket, indicating the cause of her mental state. "Need I say more? Why so many choices, each one as pretty as the next. I'll never decide!" she groused. "Now, just hand over the brownie and nobody gets hurt," she said in mock menace, and Ellie laughed along with Yasmine as she handed her the gooey confection.

Ellie's glance ran over the women gathered in the kitchen, a small smile tugging at the corners of her mouth.

Unsure of her reception by the others because of her involvement with the investigation, she'd been surprised yet pleased when Yasmine had come out to the field today and invited her to have a late lunch with the other women.

It had been a long time since the two women had seen each other, and Ellie had eagerly accepted her invitation, hoping the time spent with Yasmine and her aunt would help to keep her mind and thoughts away from Shilah.

She'd spent much of the morning as well as the

last few days in the field, continuing her work, firmly shoving all thoughts of Shilah aside when they pressed into her mind. Not that he'd made that task easy to accomplish, although he'd kept his distance from her.

It had been his nightly invasion of her dreams, some of the most erotic dreams she'd ever had, that kept him front-row-and-center in her thoughts. Dreams of herself and Shilah together, wrapped around each other, taking their passionate act to levels that even now made her blush.

The dream images of them together, bodies intertwined, locked in passion, had made sleep a restless venture at best.

The day after their encounter, hoping not to see him, Ellie hadn't known if she was relieved or disappointed when Jake, the ranch's foreman, had shown up to help instead.

For the remainder of the week Shilah had stayed away from her…and she'd been even more hyperaware of him, knowing to the *second* whenever he was anywhere in her vicinity.

Whenever he was around, the back of her neck would tingle, a slow heat invading her entire body, something she'd come to understand signaled that he was near.

She'd stop whatever she was in the process of doing and turn, seeking him out. Unable to look away, her heart would thud slowly against her rib cage as she stared across the distance at him, watching as his muscles bunched beneath his work shirt, as he handled the cattle…or the way the muscles in his throat stood out in sharp relief when he tilted his canteen to his mouth, his strong throat working down the liquid.

It was like some invisible thread connected them together—whenever he was within her general vicinity, that tingling awareness would sweep over her, and her body would respond on cue.

Her nipples would constrict and embarrassing moisture gathered in her panties.

It seemed as though even her own body was set on sabotaging her.

More than once she'd had to ask Jake or one of the other ranch hands to repeat a question they'd asked.

She had it in a bad way. And no amount of ignoring, pretending or anything else was going to make whatever she and Shilah had between them…chemistry, lust… whatever it was, go away by pretending it wasn't there.

A living, breathing entity of its own, it seemed to grow, despite her desperate attempts to pretend otherwise.

And she knew Shilah was just as aware of her. She'd felt his glance on her, more than once.

Earlier in the day she'd felt that weird tingling, one she now associated with Shilah, and had turned to see him watching her. His hot gaze brazenly skimmed over her as she sat astride her horse, the intensity, the focused way he was looking at her, bringing a wave of electric heat through her body, and she'd gasped.

Her name being called finally broke into her attention and she turned, placing a trembling smile on her face, shaken by the small encounter.

"Hmm, I don't know about the new girl, Anna," Lilly said, forcing Ellie out of her own thoughts.

"What's wrong, Aunt Lilly?" Althea asked from across the room.

This was the first time Ellie had met Nate's fiancée, Althea. From her father, Ellie had learned of Althea's history and how she'd come to Wyoming Wilde.

From what she'd learned, Althea came from money, yet her warm smile and easy personality made it seem as though Ellie had known Althea much longer than the hour they'd spent here with the women.

"Just something about her…" Lilly said, shaking her head as she dusted the flour from her hands onto her apron.

"Like what?" Althea asked, her voice distracted as she glanced over at Lilly.

Yasmine raised a brow at her aunt. "Now, Aunt Lilly…you're starting to sound like Nate!" she said, referring to her future brother-in-law and his previous mistrust of the women who worked at the ranch.

"No, it's not that," Lilly said, making a motion with her hand. "I can't quite put my finger on it." She frowned and shook her head. "Something about the way she's always sneaking around where she has no place being."

Althea bit down into the brownie, and licked away the ooze of chocolate that had escaped. "Well, if she can keep on making brownies like this…she can't be half-bad!" she said, and Ellie laughed.

"Hmm. I guess," Lilly said, her voice doubtful.

Ellie was seconds away from biting into the dessert when she felt Lilly's scrutinizing eyes on her.

"And now…why don't you tell us what's going on between you and Shilah?" she asked, and Ellie felt like a deer caught in headlights as all three women turned and looked at her, sly grins crossing their faces.

She swallowed the bite she'd taken, trying to gather her scattered wits, wondering how…what the women knew.

Chapter 12

Without having to look at his watch Shilah knew to the minute the last time he'd had sex.

And if memory served correctly, the last woman he'd been with, he'd picked up here, at the same club, while sitting on this exact same barstool.

Which was exactly why he'd come tonight.

To pick up a woman, any woman, in an attempt to ruthlessly shove away the images from his mind of Ellie, her head thrown back in ecstasy as he'd made love to her in the most intimate way.

The last moment, right before she'd climaxed, it had taken all his will not to pick her up, turn and lay her across the table, his cock embedded deep inside her sweet, willing warmth.

He inhaled a deep breath, grabbed the beer the bartender had placed in front of him, tilted his head and in one long drink, gulped down the entire contents.

Shit.

Blowing across his mind in regular rotation, much like an overplayed song on the radio whose lyrics become etched in the listener's mind, he could recall, in painful detail, every part of her soft, lusciously curved body to a T, inch by inch, curve by curve, and every nook and cranny in between.

He couldn't get her out of his mind no matter how hard he tried—no matter how many long hours he put in around the ranch, well past quitting time—the image of her, legs spread, head thrown back in bliss as he'd made love to her.

He couldn't exorcise from his mind her smell, that unique scent that seemed to belong to her and her alone, a mixture of fresh flowers and earthy woman, or the feel of her sweet lush body.

For the remainder of the week he'd kept his distance from her, his nerves so taut he knew that if he didn't, he'd say to hell with it, pick her up and carry her to his room, to pick up where they had left off.

Every day since he'd worked until he couldn't move, and finally exhausted, he'd made his way to the house, and slumped into the bed.

Where images of her continued to haunt him, relentlessly, refusing to allow him any peace of mind.

Last night, unable to take it anymore, feeling like he was losing his mind, as he'd lain in bed, staring up at the ceiling, he'd palmed his shaft in his hand, knowing that it was the only thing that would relieve the building, bone-crushing ache that was starting to drive him out of his damn mind.

He set his beer down on the counter, silently nodding

his head when the bartender asked if he wanted a refill.

Which was the only reason he was here tonight.

What was brewing between him and Ellie was something he knew wasn't good for either of them. Too many questions still lay between them, doubts and insecurities. Not to mention her dedication to maintaining her professional ethics.

But despite all of that, Shilah knew that if he continued to work side by side with her, it was only a matter of time before he'd do something stupid, and force her to admit she wanted him as badly as he wanted her.

As much as he wanted to do exactly that, in the end, he didn't want to think about how she'd feel about him afterward. Shilah lifted the beer to his lips, and this time allowed the liquid amber to slide slowly down his throat.

The arctic greeting she'd given him the next morning had shown him that her guard was back in place, a barrier she was hell-bent on maintaining between them.

With a drawn-out breath, Shilah allowed his glance to drift across the crowded bar, surveying the scene.

To hell with it. And her. If she didn't think what they had was special—if she didn't want to take the chance that what they had, what they could have, could be one of the best things that ever came their way—who was he to fight against it.

Seemed like he had been trying his whole life to prove he was worthy of someone loving him.

Forcing the maudlin thoughts to the side he continued his perusal of the club. It was Friday night, and although barely eight o'clock, the club was already hopping, as it was the hottest spot in Lander, Wyoming.

Truth be told, besides the variety of pubs on every corner, it was the only spot in town where people could dance and mingle. Sporting three levels, the club brought in customers not only in the small town of Lander, but, due to its increasing popularity, people came from miles away to party at the club.

Dubbed "the pick-up spot," it was a place where people mingled from all walks of life, all looking for a little action, if only for the night. It was a place where hookups happened regularly, and a man…or woman, was guaranteed to find someone to fill the empty void, if only for one night.

Exactly the place he needed, he thought, finishing off his beer.

There was a time when he and his brothers hit this place, or similar ones, together, the three men having their pick of women for the night. Even then, there were times when Shilah longed for something more. Something like what his brothers now had—one woman to love, to call his own, one woman he could turn to, the only one he wanted to turn to during good and bad times.

More and more, Shilah was beginning to feel like the odd man out.

Without conceit, Shilah was well aware of his effect on the opposite sex, something he and his brothers during their younger years had capitalized on.

The Wilde boys.

That's what they were called, from as young as he could remember. First, as the wild "hellions" Jed Wilde had adopted, cast-offs, unwanted by their families.

The kind of boys who, if a woman passed them on a deserted street, she would clutch her purse tightly against herself.

As the boys grew into manhood, women held on to their daughters, just as tightly.

Wilde. Undisciplined and reckless.

He and his brothers hadn't given a damn what others thought about them. He knew that, although the young girls looked at them longingly as their mothers dragged them away, Shilah and his brothers were not the types any of those same girls would dare bring home to meet their parents.

Not that it mattered.

And although their opinions had changed as they'd grown to manhood, their wealth increasing, as had their status, Shilah knew that despite all of that, if those overprotective mamas knew his history, where he'd come from, they'd turn disdainful eyes his way and swiftly hustle their daughters away.

"You here alone, sugar? Or would you like a little company?"

Shilah turned from his perusal of the club and his own thoughts to cast a slow, appraising glance over the woman who'd come to stand near the bar, next to him.

He allowed his glance to slide over her, lazily, taking in the short dress that was barely long enough to cover an ass so round and full, he wondered how she even took a step without showing her panties.

That is, if she was wearing any. He had a distinct impression that she wasn't.

The hot smile stretching across her full, red-hot lipstick-covered lips competed with her equally flaming-red hair. Although wide and inviting, there was a certain calculating look in her eyes as she in turn assessed him, head to toe.

He eyed the rest of her. The dress she wore was soft, made out of some stretchy type of material that molded her curvy body as though it were a second skin.

Despite the youthful attire and alluring smile, the heavy makeup she wore didn't disguise the fine lines that framed the corners of her mouth and eyes.

But tonight he wasn't picky. Tonight he needed a woman to take his mind away from the one he couldn't have, the one who had plagued his thoughts for longer than he wanted to admit. His cock hardened, but not for the woman standing in front of him.

She glanced down, her grin widening, and slid her glance back to meet his eyes. Moving closer, she scored the side of his face lightly with her long, sculpted nails.

"Or…we can take this party somewhere else," she suggested, her voice low, full of suggestion.

He rose from the barstool, towering over her, despite the stiletto boots she wore.

"Let's go," he said. Withdrawing his wallet, he threw down bills to cover his tab, along with a hefty tip, and turned, his arm going around the woman, and left the bar.

Chapter 13

Her hands shook as Ellie unlocked the front door and dragged her bone-weary body into her parents' home. No sooner had she closed the door than she slumped down against the frame.

She was so tired even her eyelids ached. She blew out a long breath and allowed her lids to droop as her head dropped back, leaning heavily against the door.

She would have slipped right onto the floor had she not used the last ounce of her strength to push away from the door and move farther inside the house, and slowly make her way to the kitchen.

Opening the fridge, she withdrew a large bottle of water and uncapped it, allowing the ice-cold contents to slide down her throat, closing her eyes.

She drew out a long, tired breath. The week had been one straight out of hell, with the amount of work and long hours both she and her father had put in at the clinic.

Working side by side with her father twice a week she'd helped him take care of the animals that had come to the clinic. She'd also gone along with him late one evening as he'd done his weekly visits to the small ranches in the surrounding counties, mainly doing on-site vaccinations.

Between that and her own work at the Wilde Ranch, the week had flown by in a blur.

She had the house to herself, as her parents had decided to get away for the weekend. After a lot of encouraging from Ellie—scratch that—after Ellie had *demanded* they get away, her father had taken her mother to the cabin the family owned in Jackson Hole.

Ellie's demand had come after the week of watching her father and the seemingly unending amount of energy he had as he worked from early in the morning and often long nights at the clinic.

He loved what he did, of that Ellie was certain. She'd never heard him complain about his workload. Yet over the week, far too often she'd found him relying more and more on the cane he'd starting using recently, seeing the occasional grimace cross his lined, yet still handsome face.

In addition to his own work, her father had offered to help her at the ranch. But Ellie had hastily declined his offer for the very reason she didn't want anyone involved in the ranch to assist her—the threat of bias still weighed heavy on her mind.

Besides, she'd come back home to be of help to her father, not to give him more to do.

Ellie had been torn between offering to help and

remaining silent. She, more than anyone, knew what it was like for those around her to think she was in need of help, something she'd struggled with from the time of her accident.

But it was obvious from the shadows beneath his eyes and the way he relied on his cane even more as the week had worn on that her father needed time away from the clinic, even if it was just a brief getaway.

She allowed the thought to simmer during the week. When she'd casually mentioned the idea to her mother, she'd seen the light enter her eyes. But Leandra had shaken her head, stating her father would never leave because of the clinic and his workload.

When Ellie then reminded her mother that her father was no longer alone, that she was there with him now, the smile that stretched across her mother's face had been worth the amount of work Ellie knew she'd just agreed to tackle.

Her mother had convinced her father, and Ellie couldn't have been happier seeing the surprise cross her father's face that, not only would he be getting away for a while with his beloved wife, but that his daughter would be the one to take over for him in his absence.

By the end of the week, Ellie would have paid any amount of money to get away as well, if only for a few hours, to be by herself and decompress.

The business side of the week hadn't been the only thing Ellie had been contending with, she thought, taking her bottle of water and flopping down on the sofa in the living room.

As she brought the bottle to her mouth, allowing the cold water to slip down her throat, her thoughts turned to the other reason, the one that had her up late at nights, tossing and turning, unable to get to sleep no matter how hard her day. No matter how many miles she ran she couldn't outrun the image…the memory of the way Shilah had selflessly made love to her.

Ellie finished the bottle of water and with a thud placed it on the table in front of her. Propping up her feet, she leaned back and grabbed one of her mother's throw pillows, hugging it tightly against her body.

After leaving the old cabin that day, Ellie hadn't waited for Shilah to lock up. Racing toward her horse she'd made quick work of unhitching him from the post. Ignoring the twinges of pain, she'd placed one foot in the stirrup and hoisted herself up and over the horse, settling into the saddle. Within seconds of mounting the horse she was reining it around and galloping away, before Shilah had reached her.

She'd urged the horse on faster, ignoring the shooting stabs of pain to her knee with each jostle as the large stallion ate up the distance.

She'd refused to acknowledge the mocking voice in her mind, asking who she was running from, herself or Shilah.

Once she'd reached the house, she'd dismounted.

Embarrassment, confusion and leftover lust warred for dominance in her mind. Unable to look at Shilah, to see whatever may be in his eyes when he looked at her, she began to guide the stallion toward the stable. When she felt a hand on her shoulder, she stopped but didn't look over her shoulder.

"I—I'm going to put her away," she said, running a hand over the sweat that covered the horse's back, feeling a momentary guilt that she'd pushed the horse so.

"Let me do that. You're tired. Just go home, I'll take

An Important Message from the Publisher

Dear Reader,

Because you've chosen to read one of our fine novels, I'd like to say "thank you"! And, as a special way to say thank you, I'm offering to send you two more Kimani™ Romance novels and two surprise gifts— absolutely FREE! These books will keep it real with true-to-life African American characters that turn up the heat and sizzle with passion.

Please enjoy the free books and gifts with our compliments...

Glenda Howard
For Kimani Press™

Peel off Seal and Place Inside...

K-KOM-11

We'd like to send you two free books to introduce you to Kimani™ Romance books. These novels feature strong, sexy women, and African-American heroes that are charming, loving and true. Our authors fill each page with exceptional dialogue, exciting plot twists, and enough sizzling romance to keep you riveted until the very end!

KIMANI ROMANCE...LOVE'S ULTIMATE DESTINATION

Your two books have a combined cover price of $12.50, but are yours **FREE!**

We'll even send you two wonderful surprise gifts. You can't lose!

2 FREE BONUS GIFTS!

*We'll send you two wonderful surprise gifts, (worth about $10) absolutely FREE, just for giving KIMANI™ ROMANCE books a try! Don't miss out—**MAIL THE REPLY CARD TODAY!***

Visit us online at
www.ReaderService.com

THE EDITOR'S "THANK YOU" FREE GIFTS INCLUDE:

➤ Two Kimani™ Romance Novels
➤ Two exciting surprise gifts

YES! I have placed my Editor's "thank you" Free Gifts seal in the space provided at right. Please send me 2 FREE books, and my 2 FREE Mystery Gifts. I understand that I am under no obligation to purchase anything further, as explained on the back of this card.

PLACE
FREE GIFTS
SEAL
HERE

About how many NEW paperback fiction books have you purchased in the past 3 months?

❏ 0-2   ❏ 3-6   ❏ 7 or more

FDCD   FDCP   FDCZ

168/368 XDL

Please Print

FIRST NAME

LAST NAME

ADDRESS

APT.#   CITY

STATE/PROV.   ZIP/POSTAL CODE

Thank You!

care of everything," he said. And for a brief moment she stood there, facing away from him. She bit her lip in indecision, fighting against the urge to turn and face him, to get it all out, and answer his question.

But in the end she didn't, she couldn't. She didn't know the answers herself.

She waited for him to say more. Waited until the tension grew so thick, she felt its invisible hands reach out as though to choke her.

Close to tears, unreasonable, crazy tears, she'd silently nodded her head and had nearly run to her car.

The morning after their hot, tumultuous lovemaking at the cabin, Ellie hadn't expected to see Shilah at all, much less have him show up before she had arrived. Already at work with the men, he'd been herding the cattle and tagging them, waiting for Ellie's arrival.

Although to the casual observer Ellie doubted anything had seemed wrong as business had returned to usual, she had felt the strain between her and Shilah. She'd been jumpy the entire day, waiting...expecting, and yes, she admitted to herself, there was a part of her that wanted him to bring up what had happened.

Ellie laughed, without humor, and rose from the sofa, making her way to her bedroom. Obviously it hadn't meant to him what it had meant to her. Not only had he not mentioned it, but the following day, as well as the rest of the week, Jake had taken his place.

But why should it mean anything to him, what they'd done, she thought. Shilah, as well as all his brothers, had never been short of female attention. Although discriminate in his bed partners even when they were teens, Ellie had been aware, painfully so, of that fact.

Padding naked to the bathroom, she started the shower

and turned to grab her essentials. She paused when her eyes met her reflection, allowing the towel she'd wrapped around her body to slip as she ran a critical glance over her body.

All legs, that's what her father used to say about her, growing up.

She was nothing but long legs and lean lines. She ran a hand over her body, stopping at her breasts. Small, they barely spilled over her hands.

She drew in a breath, remembering the feel of Shilah's hands as they had lightly grazed over them.

Shame brought a blush over her face as she thought of the wanton way she'd pressed into his hands, silently asking…begging for him to touch her, to sooth away the ache that had been growing steadily since the moment they'd re-connected.

She thumbed a finger over her nipple, watching in fascination as it sprang tightly against her thumb. Her breathing grew ragged, as she thought of the contrast of feeling between his callused hand and soft touch as it had brushed over her.

Her hand trailed down the line of her flat stomach. She hesitated, her hand hovering over her mound. She glanced up at the mirror and her reflection shocked her.

Hastily she turned from the mirror, and jumped into the shower, allowing the cold water to rain over her over-heated skin.

Chapter 14

Shilah killed the engine on his truck and sat behind the steering wheel, contemplating his next move.

Or better yet, why the hell he was here. His glance fell to the time on his dash…almost midnight, outside Ellie Crandall's parents' home. He turned and glanced at his passenger seat.

Like some lovesick calf, he sat staring at the flowers, afraid to go and knock on her door before turning away and running a hand through his hair.

Yeah, he knew the flowers were clichéd as hell. But, after driving around downtown Lander for over an hour, knowing he should just go home and call it a night, every time he made the turn down the road that would lead out of town, he found himself turning right back and making the circuit around the small downtown area again.

If he had any damn sense he'd be at a motel some-where, holed up with the willing redhead from the club, losing himself inside her warm, willing body to ease the painful throb of his cock.

The need that was growing to the point that he thought he'd lose his mind if he didn't assuage the ache soon, waking up every morning fisting his cock, images of Ellie burning in his mind.

Only to face the woman responsible for putting him in his current state, forced to pretend that what they'd shared hadn't happened. That it didn't mean a damn thing to him.

If he had any sense, he'd be right in the middle of plunging inside the woman…Jenny, Janie…hell, he hadn't even remembered her name. But, names weren't important. The only thing that was important was hearing her softness as her moans and sighs of delight bounced off the walls, as he lost himself inside her body, forcing any lingering thoughts…wants or desires for Ellie from his mind.

But, he'd been denied even that solace.

As soon as he'd ushered the woman out of the club, the wind had stirred, blowing her cloying perfume across his nose, and he'd paused, glancing down at the woman, whose arm was wrapped around his waist like a cobra.

The memory of an earthy yet wildly feminine scent had chosen that moment to assault his mind, drawing a deep breath from him.

He'd stopped, his arm draped loosely around the woman's shoulders, and inhaled as though to recapture the scent.

What he should have been doing, what he could

have been doing was a far cry from what had happened instead.

He'd cursed and the woman...Jenny, Janie...had looked up at him, a question in her light blue eyes.

No matter how badly he wanted...needed sex, his body on fire, his need running high, it wasn't an anonymous woman he wanted; a stranger to spend the night with.

His longing had nothing to do with easing the painful throb of his cock with the simple act of sex.

The need he had was for one woman and one woman alone.

Despite the hot promise in her eyes of what was to come, or the way her ample curves pressed into his side, he'd mumbled an excuse and without a word turned and strode toward his car.

The only woman he wanted was Ellie and no other would do.

Whatever was between him and Ellie wasn't going to go away anytime soon. And if he wanted any kind of return of his sanity, he had to do something about it. Now.

The last week had proven that. If anything, it was only getting stronger. He'd tried, tried like hell to do the noble thing, give her some space and let her come to the same realization. But, after a week of torture, he couldn't take it anymore.

He was claiming her.

He didn't know what would happen with them, but he wanted to give them a chance, and if he left it up to her neither one of them would ever know if what they had was real.

He turned, lifted the flowers from the seat and strode toward her door.

* * *

Ellie groaned out loud, dragged out of a deep sleep by an insistent pounding.

She hissed, clutching the sides of her head with her hands, trying to block out the pounding to know avail.

She opened one eye and glanced down, barely lifting her head.

She was lying on the sofa, the empty bottle lying next to her, on the floor.

"Innocent, my foot," she mumbled, groaning as she plopped back down on the sofa.

Her last memory had been of leaving the shower and going to bed.

Despite how tired she was, sleep had eluded her, and with a sigh she'd risen from bed and wearily stomped down the stairs to the main floor.

She'd gone into the kitchen, rummaging through first the pantry and then the refrigerator looking for something, anything, that would help her go to sleep.

She never had been much for using drugs, even the more innocent variety bought over the counter. She steered away from them, despite the occasional bouts of insomnia she'd suffered, dating back to her teen years. But the sleeplessness had never been so bad that a little herbal tea hadn't been able to cure it.

Her mother had always made sure to keep plenty of herbal tea available, then and now, just in case. She'd sighed in relief when she'd found a carton, soon groaning when it was empty.

Just about ready to don her sneakers and head out to the Quick Mart near her parents' house, she spied a six-pack of mixed cocktails, tucked away on a back shelf.

With a shrug of her shoulders, she'd tugged a single bottle from the pack, thinking that right about then, she'd do anything to quell the mental gymnastics she'd been having, as thoughts of Shilah had been playing hell with her ability to go to sleep.

The pounding stopped momentarily and she sighed in relief only to groan as it returned, this time so loud she felt as though her head was about to crack open.

Her eyes flew open. The pounding she heard was not coming from the little sadistic man inside her head, but from the front door.

With a loud moan she pushed herself away from the sofa. She kept her head steady against the slight throbbing that was competing with a vengeance with the pounding that was coming from the front door.

"I'm coming, I'm coming! Hold on," she grumbled, frowning as she glanced toward the cable box on top of the television, the glowing numbers indicating the lateness of the hour.

At nearly midnight, Ellie wondered who was banging on the door as if they'd lost their mind, hoping against hope that it wasn't some type of emergency from one of her father's clients that would require her attention.

Swiftly pulling her hair from the ragged ponytail she'd secured it with earlier, she jogged toward the front door. "I'm sorry it took so long, I was—"

Not thinking, she opened the door without benefit of peeking through the hole to see who her midnight caller was, something she immediately wanted to slap herself silly for after swinging the door open.

Her sentence trailed off when her glance came into

contact with the one man she hadn't expected to see on her doorstep.

Not to mention the huge bouquet of flowers he held in his hand.

The scowl on his face was in direct contrast with the look of…uncertainty, hesitancy in his dark eyes.

"I, uh, got these for you."

Ellie looked from Shilah to the flowers wrapped in green tissue that he held tightly in his hand. It was so corny, so clichéd that she should have closed the door in his face and walked away.

She glanced at the flowers, an artful arrangement of pink mini-carnations mixed with pink roses. Both her favorite flowers.

She should close the door, but she didn't. Her eyes went to his.

The hesitant look in his beautiful eyes, coupled with the contrasting feelings she'd been teeter-tottering with the entire week, playing hell with her ability to concentrate, were her undoing.

"Thank you," she said, the words in no way expressing how she felt, yet all she could manage to say.

Instead of saying anything more for fear she'd embarrass herself, she instead buried her face inside the fragrant bouquet again, taking a deep appreciative breath as the soft petals tickled her nose.

"I hoped you'd like them," he said, and her eyes went to his, to see him staring at her with an intensity that shook her.

"Please…let me come in, Ellie."

Ellie gave in to the inevitable, nodded her head shortly and opened the door wider, allowing him to enter.

The light that entered his eyes was hot, intense, searing. Ellie felt her heart strum in both anticipation and fear and wondered if how she felt was anything like what Little Red must have felt when she walked into the wolf's den.

Chapter 15

He trailed her to the kitchen. No sooner had she opened a cabinet drawer, than he spoke.

"I haven't been able to get you…us, what we did, out of my mind, Ellie. No matter how hard I try. No matter what limitations you put on us."

Ellie became still, briefly, before she continued searching for a vase.

She barely refrained from spinning around to challenge him.

But, after all the mental gymnastics she'd been going through over the last few days, torn between giving in to what his eyes promised he wanted from her, as well as memories of their lovemaking, she'd been barely keeping it together. In doing so she had kept her distance from him, forcing him to do the same.

"And I don't think you have, either," he said, quietly.

Her hands held a fine tremor as she flipped on the faucet and began to fill the vase, without responding to him.

The tension mounted in the semidark room as the silence grew. When she'd brought him into the house, she hadn't bothered turning on any additional lights, her intending for his stay to be short.

But now, the low lights from the single lamp in the living room and the light above the stove lent an intimacy to the room she didn't want or need. His mere presence alone was enough to play havoc with her mind and libido.

Ellie knew that she could give in to what was growing between them. She could give in to the promises he'd given her when they'd made love, a promise to fulfill every fantasy she'd ever created about them.

Give in to the heat that had been growing between them since she'd returned, so intense it was now a living breathing entity of its own.

It didn't matter if anyone was around them, whenever they were near each other, made the slightest brush of contact either physically or just with their eyes, everything else faded away and it was only the two of them.

Yes, he was right. Something had to give.

But the other end of that was what would happen to her, when it was over.

The flowers in her hand forgotten, she turned to face him. "Limitations? What limitations have I forced on you, Shilah?"

He shoved away from the wall where he'd been leaning, making his way toward her, running his eyes over her.

He was staring at her as though he read her every thought. As though he knew her every secret desire.

Unable to turn away she helplessly watched his approach.

She forced herself to move, turning back around to finish placing the flowers in the vase. "I don't know what you're talking about. I haven't placed any limitations on us...on you, any more so than what should be there."

He stopped and, although she couldn't see him, Ellie could *feel* him, the warmth from his body reaching out to enfold her in its embrace.

She inhaled, deeply. His unique masculine scent overpowered the scent of the flowers, hitting her at once, and she closed her eyes, feeling her nipples pearl behind her gown in reaction to his nearness.

He hadn't even touched her, yet her body betrayed her, tingling head to toe.

She felt his hand on her shoulder, the warmth seeping through the thin cotton of her gown, and bit her bottom lip.

"What is it that scares you, Ellie?"

She was silent, trying to figure out in her mind what...how to answer a question that she didn't know the answer to. He'd asked her that question before. Just as she hadn't known the answer then, neither did she now.

To deny that she was afraid...well, that was no longer an option. Not only did he know her too well, she couldn't give voice to the lie even to herself.

She felt him move closer, crowding her space, until her legs bumped up against the counter.

"What would happen if you just gave in, Ellie?" The forbidden words were whispered against her temple and Ellie felt her heart pound against her chest in a slow, hard beat, each one she heard...felt, throbbing.

"Shilah, if I did…what if—" she stopped, swallowed and felt him step impossibly closer, until she felt the coarse material of his jeans brush against the backs of her legs.

He turned her around to face him.

His nearness blocked out sound, sight, smell…until it was only him that she saw, everything in the room, everything she'd ever felt it seemed before she'd met him, before this moment, faded away as though it had never been.

She closed her eyes.

"Trust me," he said, and lowered his mouth, his lips brushing against hers in a soft, seesawing motion. She felt the response of the small touch shoot through her body like fire.

He licked the corner of her lip.

Ellie's nipples constricted against the thin gown she wore, painfully.

"Trust me, Ellie. Like you always have."

She placed a hand against his chest and forced him to move away, so that she could see his face. Dark eyes stared down at her, searching hers.

"I've never done this—" She stopped, gestured with one hand in a sweeping motion. "Before."

Shilah frowned, "And by this you mean…" He allowed the sentence to dangle.

"This type of relationship. One where I don't know what's going to happen. Don't really know the boundaries," she finished lamely.

"Do we have to know what's going to happen? Does everything in your life have to go according to your clipboard?" he asked, and she caught the teasing glint in his dark eyes.

She shook her head. "No, but I like to know what I'm getting into before I jump into the fire," she murmured.

"I'll be there to catch you, before you get burned, Ellie."

Ellie was afraid it was too late for that. He'd burned her with his touch, seared and branded her the first moment their mouths had met.

Long minutes and several drugging kisses later, Ellie broke away from him, her breathing heavy.

"Baby, what's wrong?" he asked, hearing the tremble in his own voice.

He was on fire with need for her. He pulled her close and bent as though to bring their mouths back into contact.

She'd asked what he wanted from her. His hand came up to frame her face, his thumbs caressing her cheeks, running over her face, down the length of her neck. He spanned the hollow of her throat, feeling her heartbeat jump against his fingers.

The move he knew, boldly possessive.

Staking his claim.

Ellie placed her hand on his chest, shoving at him, yet with not as much strength as before.

Their eyes locked in a heated battle of wills, even as desire and lust—and something more, something he willed her to see—were a hazy cloud engulfing them.

"Not...not here." The words seemed torn from her. "Not at my parents' house," she finished, and relief flooded him.

Despite the painful throb of his erection, he ruthlessly shoved down the need to pick her up, carry her to the nearest soft spot and make love to her until neither one of them could think straight, until she could voice no more objections to him as she lay spent and sated beneath him.

He drew in a shaky breath and nodded his head, his eyes searching hers.

"Then come home with me, Ellie. Come home with me and make love to me."

Chapter 16

Although he'd wanted her to drive with him, Ellie had followed Shilah, using the time alone to gather her thoughts, analyze what she was doing and why.

When all else failed, she fell back on her reasoning… her way of analyzing things to help her understand. She thought of every reason she shouldn't be in her car at midnight following Shilah Wilde back to his place. She thought of how easy she'd given in to him, how easily she'd agreed to come home with him.

Simply because he'd asked.

All of her analyzing came to a halt. He'd only had to ask and she'd followed him.

She wanted him. Wanted this night with him. A night she knew would bring her the kind of pleasure she'd never known before. The kind of pleasure she'd never allowed herself to feel with another.

As she parked her car next to his in the driveway, before she could open her car door he was there beside her, helping her out, taking the bag she'd hastily packed, and ushering her to the house.

Although it was late and she knew the likelihood that anyone was awake to see her late-night creeping, she sighed in relief when he took her around the back entry.

"We each have our own entry. Something we had the construction crew do a few years ago," he said by way of explanation, yet Ellie knew he was using the entry for her benefit.

They'd barely walked inside before he turned to her.

"Tell me," he said, pulling a frown from Ellie.

"Tell you...tell you what?" she asked, her voice halting, her eyes trained on the full lower rim of his sensual mouth.

He leaned down and placed a kiss on her mouth, before withdrawing.

"Tell me." His command was made in a voice no louder than before, yet she heard the steely demand.

She knew what he wanted. He wanted her to admit that she wanted him as much as he wanted her.

To admit that thoughts of him had stayed with her, night and day, from the moment they'd made love in the old shack.

To admit that she wanted him in every carnal way that his eyes promised he wanted her.

As he stood staring down at her from beneath hooded lids, his face tightened as the hand that had been caressing her face slipped down and opened, wrapping loosely around her throat, the hold subtle but possessive.

"I—I want you, Shilah." She forced the admission from the tight constriction in her throat.

At her answer, she felt his anger and, confused, she glanced up at him, wondering what he wanted from her.

"What do you want from me?" she cried. "I'm here, I can't give you anything else, Shilah. Not now," she said, knowing the answer she gave wasn't the one he wanted.

She turned away, her hand on the knob. "This was a mistake, I—"

Before she could turn the knob he spun her back around, the light in his eyes frightening her in its intensity.

"No man has ever made me feel like you have, Shilah," she said, fighting against the need to cry. "So—" She threw her hands up in the air, at a loss for words.

"Needed. Wanted." He finished tilting her head to force her to look at him.

She licked the bottom of her lip, and nodded her head wordlessly.

As his gaze traveled over her face, she saw the slight flare of his nostrils.

The admission hadn't been easy and was one she tried not to think about, kept hidden deep inside in that place she held away from others.

"You don't have to hold back from me, Ellie. You don't have to protect yourself."

It was as though he'd pushed down past the layers… the barriers she'd erected between herself and others and pulled out the very heart of who she was.

"I—" She opened her mouth to speak and he laid a finger over her mouth, silencing her.

"Don't say, Ellie. Just feel."

"Yes."

Without another word, Shilah's hands went to work, roaming over her body, down her legs until he reached the hem of her skirt. Slowly he eased her skirt up and away from her legs. The material sliding along her bare thighs, combined with the touch of his hands against her overly sensitive skin, elicited a deep shiver from Ellie.

He deftly unzipped the back of her skirt, tugging it down her legs and kicking it to the side, sliding his hot, hard hands along her waist until he reached her panties.

Lowering his head, he covered her mouth with his, swallowing her moans. His fingers brushed across along the damp crotch of her panties, eliciting a deep moan from Ellie.

His mouth was hard, unforgiving in its demands as he plunged his tongue deep inside her mouth. Yet his fingers deftly worked at her panties until with an impatient tug he ripped them from her body.

When he placed one lone finger deep inside her body, already wet for him, he broke away from her groaning against her lips. "So wet...so sweet," he groaned against her mouth.

Shilah's finger delved within her slick folds and pushed inside her warm, wet sheath, groaning harshly when her greedy walls clenched and tightened on his fingers, her lean but lush body grinding against him.

His shaft swelled to painful proportions when he thought of how snugly she'd fit, wrapped around him.

Her low moans filled his room, echoing off the walls when he slowly dragged his finger in and out of her tight sheath, before slowly dragging his finger completely out of her body.

His breathing was heavy, his heart thudding against his ribs. He brought his finger up to see her essence covering the single digit. He kept his gaze steady on hers as he brought his finger to his mouth and struck his tongue out to clean it of her cream.

His cock jumped, pressing hotly against her naked mound, and he brought his hand down and grasped hers from where it rested against his chest.

He brought their joined hands between their bodies, wrapping her small hand around his shaft to show her what she did to him with just one taste of her.

His nostrils flared at the light that entered her dark eyes, one that spoke of feminine triumph at what she'd done to him.

With a growl he lifted her, straddling her legs around his waist, and backed her to the bed, laying her down in the center and covering her body with his.

He slid his hand between their bodies, impatiently tugging on her shirt, deftly lifting it up and over her head to drop over the side of the bed.

As she'd dressed to come home with him, she hadn't bothered putting on a bra, and her perfect round breasts were bared to his gaze.

He leaned down, cupped one of the small mounds in one hand and stroked his thumb over the nipple. With a tight groan he replaced his thumb with his tongue, scraping it over and over until it spiked, before pulling it deep inside his mouth.

Her nipple scraped the underside of his mouth as he laved it in long, sweeping moves, before clamping his teeth down on her nipple, suckling and tugging on it, mimicking what he was doing with his fingers with the bud of her femininity.

"Shilah..." she panted, mewling, the sound an utterly feminine one, as she ground herself against his mouth and fingers.

His shaft hardened to granite, yet he took his time with her, playing and toying with her to bring her to the brink of orgasm only to retreat, his fingers pinching her clitoris while they spread her own moisture over and around her pearl of femininity.

"Shilah, Shilah, please," she cried, her body moving against his, her breath coming out in harsh gasps of air as he continued to work her.

Past the haze of lust he glanced down at her, her body trembling, her head thrown back as she moaned out her pleasure.

The position of her body on his, the way she moved against him and her little cries were his undoing. Unable to take it any further, he tore away from her, and quickly rose, shedding his clothes. As she lay in the center of the bed, her dark eyes followed him, watching his every move as he then reached inside the bedside table and lifted a small foil wrapper from inside.

Once fully sheathed he turned back to face her, and stopped, his heart thudding violently against his chest as he viewed her as she lay sprawled on his bed.

The moon's beams rained from the skylight in his ceiling, casting an almost ethereal glow over her deep chocolate-colored skin, lying naked, decadently sprawled out on his bed.

Her hair was a messy tangle, mostly from his hands as they'd shifted through the strands as they'd kissed.

It obscured part of her face, yet he could feel her eyes on him in the dark.

God, she was beautiful. No matter how often he'd imagined this scene, her body bared completely to him, never in his wildest imagination had Shilah imagined she'd look like this.

With her elbows propped behind her, her upper torso was slightly bowed; her small round breasts were thrust forward.

His glance trailed over them, across her dark, chocolate-colored nipples that under his ardent gaze spiked long, taut…begging for his kisses.

Shilah was more than happy to oblige.

As he moved back to the bed, she rose and met him, her hand coming out hesitantly to run over his length, shocking a deep moan from him.

He'd allowed her soft, almost innocent touch as she'd wrapped her hand around his cock, her hands so slender and small, she'd barely been able to circle him.

When she'd squeezed, he'd groaned, moving her away, pushing her down on the bed, his body moving to cover hers again.

"If I let you do that now, baby, this will be over before it starts," he said roughly. He caught the blush that stained her pretty cheeks when she realized what he meant.

"Soon enough, El. Soon enough you can touch me all you want. But this time around belongs to me."

He moved into the V of her legs, his erection pressing against the moist nook of her femininity.

"Shilah," she whispered, as he nuzzled the skin directly behind her ear, knowing it was one of her hot spots.

He groaned as her sweet body molded to his, her

arms creeping out to wrap around his neck and pull him closer.

It seemed like an eternity that he'd wanted to feel her…taste her. He took a deep breath, inhaling her unique smell deep into his lungs.

"I love your skin, Ellie," he whispered against her throat before his tongue snaked out and licked the hollow.

"So smooth…decadent rich chocolate."

"Thank…thank you," she whispered huskily, a catch in her throat. He pushed away enough so that he could see her face. His gaze went over her passion-stamped face, lips swollen from his kisses, lids droopy, as she returned his gaze.

He leaned down again, dragging his mouth across the valley between her breasts, swirling and suckling a nipple, alternating his attention between both.

As badly as he wanted to spread her thighs and plunge deep inside her warm, tight sheath, he desired to draw out the pleasure, a pleasure it had seemed an eternity he had dreamed about, yearned for.

Ellie's body bowed sharply when he pulled one of her hardened nipples into the hot cavern of his mouth and suckled her, hard.

Each decadent glide of his tongue against her breasts, every tug and pull against her aching nipples sent her essence down her thigh.

When he pulled away from her, her eyes flew open as she clutched at his wide shoulders, silently begging him to return.

He licked a path up her body, ending at her mouth

and whispered. "Do you like what I'm doing to you, Ellie?"

Ellie nodded her head up and down, speech beyond her at the moment as he catered to her every decadent whim.

When she'd seen him, naked, as he'd turned to face her, his shaft thick and long, hanging between his thick thighs, a sharp pang of desire had furled low in her belly, snaking through her body, striking her as swiftly as a boa constrictor and leaving her just as breathless.

She'd thought him sinfully gorgeous before, fully clothed...but goodness. It was nothing compared to seeing him bared, standing before her, hard and ready. Just for her.

"Are you ready for me?" he asked, biting down on her nipple, not hard enough to hurt, but enough that she felt the sting, trailing a hot path from her nipple to the core of her.

Her head tossed on the pillow, as she moaned and cried, asking...no, shamelessly begging him to give her what she needed so desperately.

She heard his low, masculine laugh, and seconds later he was easing back between her legs. Pressing her thighs wide, he lifted them at the bend of her knee.

She inhaled a startled breath, her eyes widening in alarm when she felt the broad tip of his penis poised against her entry.

Within moments of her consent, he was feeding her his shaft, inch by torrid inch, until Ellie gasped, grabbing onto his thick forearms and sinking her nails deep, scoring his flesh.

"Ohh," she hissed. "Shilah...Shilah, you're...big,"

she rushed out, embarrassed. But forced to admit the truth she continued, the words halting. "And…it's been a while for me. A long while. Just, give me…give me a minute."

She felt his arms that held her legs wide tremble, yet he leaned down to place a kiss on her mouth.

"We'll go at your pace, baby," he promised.

As before, Elli was struck by his utter selflessness. One she knew didn't come easy, as she felt the hardness between her legs give testimony.

He reached his hand between her legs, lightly stroking her clitoris, until she felt the tension ease from her body, as her body again readied itself for him.

After several tense moments she took a deep breath, and nodded her head for him to continue. Slowly he continued to feed her his shaft, carefully, until he was fully seated inside her body, his sac tapping against the soft space between her bottom and the lips of her vagina and they released mutual sounds of pleasure.

Yet, it wasn't until she told him verbally she was okay that he moved, adjusting her so that she lay snugly against him.

Her mouth opened in an O of surprise when, without losing connection, he shifted them so that she lay sprawled on top of him.

"You control the ride, baby," Shilah said, staring up at her beautiful body as she lay on top of him. "I—I don't want to hurt you. And your pleasure is my main goal. My only desire."

As she sat astride him, Shilah was forced to shut his eyes against the sight of her, one side of her mouth hitching in the smile he favored that brought out her lone dimple, afraid, as he'd told her, it would be over before it started.

As she rode him, he glanced up at her from hooded eyes, watching as her small breasts slapped together with every bounce and glide.

Her eyes were closed and she was biting down into the lower rim of her lip as she established a rhythm, one he had allowed her to set, and one that had him clenching his jaw, fighting down the need to flip her over and dive into her over and over, until he'd wrung every bit of release from her lithe body.

Ellie was on fire.

Shilah's hard hands dug deep grooves into her waist as he held her tight. Squirming against him, her body was on fire as the decadent, delicious pressure build inside her with every hard driving drag and pull of his shaft inside her body.

But, it wasn't enough.

She couldn't get close enough to him, and felt crazed with the need for a release she felt, hovering, just out of reach.

When he placed a hand between them, and found her clit, pinching it lightly, spreading her own essence between the seam of her lips as she feverishly worked her body against his, she released a low keening moan, her body quickening its pace.

He swiftly removed his hand, placing it on her backside, and urged her to go faster, quickening the pace and Ellie felt every muscle in her body tense, as she arched her body and screamed her release.

Within minutes of her wrenching cries of release,

her body shaking uncontrollably, she felt him shift their bodies so that she lay beneath him.

Thinking she had nothing else to give, her body weak from her orgasm, she lay on the bed, spent.

When he spread her thighs, repositioned himself between them, she offered only a groan, too weak to do anything else.

He grasped both of her wrists, shackling them with one of his hands, and drove back inside, so deep, it wrung a deep moan from Ellie. So deep she felt him stroke the back of her womb.

Thinking she had no more to give, he proved her wrong, driving into her over and over with surefire strokes, and she felt the delicious curl of pressure build this time deep, deep inside her body.

"Do you want to come with me, again…to that place just for us?" he whispered the decadent words against her ear, and mindless with pleasure she bobbed her head up and down.

"Then come for me, again, Ellie…come with me," he said.

When he lifted her leg, leveling her at a different angle against his shaft and drove inside her, she broke, her keening cries of release echoing off the wall.

Their cries of release, one low, harsh and deep, the other high, wailing, merged into one harmonious cry of satisfaction as together they gave over and their cries blended into one long, unanimous cry of satisfaction.

Chapter 17

You can ring my be-e-ell, ring my bell, ring my bell ring-a-ling-a-ling!

Although muffled, the sound of her alarm from her phone brought Ellie out of a deep sleep and she groaned, mentally cursing herself.

She'd forgotten to change the setting on her phone so that the damn thing didn't go off on Sunday, the *only* day of the week that she didn't have to get up at o-dark-thirty.

When Ellie raised her arms above her head, arching her back as she did so, she stopped, mid-yawn, and slowly expelled, finishing the yawn in one long breath.

She slowly pried open eyes that felt filled with sand, swallowing deeply.

Oh God...please don't let that be...

No amount of praying was going to remove the large

male arm that was draped around her waist…nor the big hand that cupped her butt.

She swiftly closed her eyes, hoping—praying—that last night had been nothing more than a result of a very hot dream.

A wildly erotic, out of this world dream, but please… just a dream.

She closed her eyes, vainly hoping that when she opened them, he would be gone and she'd be left alone in her bed at home. Slowly she counted to ten. Twenty. Hmm…thirty. Slowly.

When she opened her eyes again, not only was he still there, but he was lying next to her, his head braced on his elbow as he stared down at her, one side of his sensual mouth hitched in a low, wicked smile.

The same kind of smile that had gotten her in trouble in the first place.

"Hey, you," he said, in a sexy growl, his deep voice roughened with sleep, one finger coming out to lightly caress the side of her face.

Ellie cleared her throat, staring up at him. "Hey, you," she replied, clearing her throat, hearing a similar gruffness. On Shilah it was sexy and oh-so-hot, but on her, she managed to sound like a frog.

When he bent his head down to kiss her, Ellie raised her hand, connecting with his hard, naked chest, turning her face to the side before he could make contact.

"Shilah," she said, drawing in a hissing breath when she felt his wicked tongue snake a path with its tip down her neck, running along her collarbone and back up.

"We shouldn't." She shook her head, rephrasing her wording. "We *can't*. Last night…last night was a mistake, a mistake that can't happen again."

As she spoke she could feel the hard length of his naked shaft as it lay against her thigh, and his hand that had been lightly cupping her butt moved, trailing along on her hip to softly tangle in the hair covering her mound.

"Shilah…Shilah, I'm serious. We can't do this," she said, twisting her body to try and evade his busy hands and searching mouth.

She yelped out a surprise when he smoothly flipped their bodies so that she lay beneath him, trapped, his arms coming out like brackets on either side of her, effectively caging her in.

"No, you're right, Ellie. We can't…because you seem hell-bent on making sure that doesn't happen."

She twisted around, squirming beneath him, glaring up at him. "Let me out of here, Shilah. I need to go home—"

His mouth came down hard on hers and she stubbornly kept her lips closed, refusing to give in to his demand.

He moved his hands from where they shackled her body, and brought his hands up to her face, his kiss gentling until, with a soft cry, Ellie gave in to the softness of his kiss.

Slowly he lifted his head, his dark eyes staring down at her, intensely. Ellie sighed, looking away from him.

"What's wrong, Ellie?" he asked, moving away from her. He shifted their bodies so that she lay in front of him, with his arms coming out to cross over her.

Naturally, as though they had lain that way together for years, her body fitted into the groove of his embrace as though that's what it had been made to do.

As Shilah listened to Ellie speak, her voice hesitant at first, as she outlined all the reasons why they shouldn't be together, outlined all the reasons why what they'd done last night was wrong, he finally stopped her, pulling her around to face him.

"Listen, none of that matters, Ellie. None of those are good enough reasons for me to stay away from you," he said, and saw the indecision in her eyes. "For you to deny what we have—" he stopped, cupping her face in his palms "—is real or that it shouldn't have happened... that what we have growing between us isn't something worth breaking a few rules for is..." He stopped again hearing the catch in his own voice.

"I can't do that, Ellie...even for you."

"Shilah, this has all happened so fast. We barely know each other—"

"What are you talking about, El?" he broke in, frowning. "We've known each other all our lives," he said, shaking his head.

"As children, yes, Shilah." She spoke softly, and Shilah heard the emotion that made her voice shaky.

"Ellie, can you tell me that you don't have feelings for me now? Feelings that go beyond what we felt when we were kids?" Shilah knew his voice was pleading, but he didn't give a damn. She meant more to him than any woman ever had. She always had.

She always would.

She turned away, but not before he saw the glimmer of tears in her beautiful light brown eyes. She sniffed and nodded her head slightly.

"You know I do," she replied softly. At her admission he went to pull her closer. She shook her head and again he felt his heart thud heavily against his chest, reading the rejection in her eyes.

"But—" She stopped and took a deep breath. "Despite any feelings, I…we…can't do this."

Forcing her to face him, he brought her close, and laid a soft kiss against her lips.

"All I'm asking for is a chance, Ellie, before you throw away something that could be good…damn good. Something special. Just give us a chance. That's all I'm asking."

"Shilah, my job…I can't allow this to interfere. There are ethical issues I have to consider—"

He laid a kiss on her mouth and slowly withdrew. "I'm willing to wait, El. No pressure."

She frowned up at him, her brows drawn together. "No pressure…okay, what exactly are you saying?"

"Until you finish the investigation, I'll back off."

Ellie stared up at him, worrying her bottom lip with her teeth. "Meaning exactly…?" she asked, holding her breath. As much as she wanted to explore what they had…what they could have, she wasn't willing to risk everything she'd worked hard for. Even for Shilah.

The sexy half smile that hitched the corners of his mouth upward was almost her undoing.

For a brief moment she was tempted to say to hell with it, throw consequences to the wind, and go with what her heart was telling her was the best thing that ever happened to her.

She drew in a deep breath, waiting for his answer.

"Ellie, I know your job…your career is important to you. And it's important to me, too. If you think my helping you could in any way jeopardize your professionalism, baby, you've got to know you mean too much to me for me to allow that. I'll have Jake take over for me, until you finish.

"And…" He drew in a deep breath. "Until this is over, and you've sent in your report, I'll back off personally, as well," he promised.

Ellie's face broke into a wide grin at his answer.

"I hope that happy Cheshire-cat grin on your face isn't because I'm backing off…that's only temporary."

"Just like that?"

He grabbed her and, pulling her body on top of his, lay claim to her lips.

"Yep, just like that," he said, after giving her a pulse-pounding kiss. "But don't get used to it," he said a frown marring his perfect features. But, she saw the twinkle in his unique eyes. "As soon as this is over…the very minute you tell me you've completed your assignment, I'm claiming what's mine."

The sensual threat in his tone sent a delicious curl of heat along Ellie's body. Not to mention the feel of his shaft, long, deliciously hard, as it pressed against her heat.

"So what do you want to do about this?" she said, moving her brows up and down suggestively while wiggling her hips against him.

All humor vanished when he placed his hands on her rear and flipped them so that she lay sprawled beneath him.

"One more time won't hurt, will it? Give me something to tide me over while I'm waiting," he said in a deep, *do me, baby* voice.

With a feminine purr of acquiescence she softly ground herself against him.

"I'm going to take that as a yes," he said with a groan,

completely covering her body with his as he did his best to make sure the experience would indeed tide them over until they could be together, again.

Chapter 18

"Dr. Crandall, what do you want us to do with the livestock we have in the south pasture? They're new, haven't been mingling with the others yet...are they s'posed to be quarantined, too?"

Ellie broke her attention away from her notes, where she'd been scribbling down the *last* of her observations for the last pen of animals, and stretched her back.

It had been a long day, and her body was feeling the effects, the muscles in her back bunching and tensing. Yet, the end was near and soon she'd complete her investigation.

Although she and Shilah had been careful to keep their distance from each other, Ellie had caught the looks from the others when they thought she wasn't looking. Somehow, word had gotten around about them.

Not that it had taken a rocket scientist to figure it out,

she reflected, worrying the lower rim of her lip at the nagging thought.

Shilah had been true to his word, keeping his distance from her as she worked, allowing Jake to take over for him as Ellie finished her investigation.

At times she wondered if the agreed separation was becoming as difficult for him as it was for her. Last night, after watering and feeding her favorite stallion following her customary ride once she'd finished work, he'd shown her, explicitly, that she wasn't alone.

As she'd turned, leaving the stable, Shilah had been there.

Before she could speak, he'd placed a finger over her mouth, shushing her, and had proceeded to dispel any lingering doubts in her mind that their separation wasn't as hard on him as it was for her.

After their short but hot tryst, they'd left the stable together, and had run into two of the ranch hands, along with the young girl who'd helped Lilly in the kitchen.

Although she'd feigned nonchalance, swiftly walking away from Shilah, a nagging feeling settled deep in Ellie's stomach as she'd wondered if they'd seen what the two of them had been doing.

"What do you think, Mom? Too much?" Ellie asked, turning in the full-length cheval mirror to look at herself from all angles.

She'd gone through her entire wardrobe, twice, and tried on every combination of outfits until finally settling on the closest thing she had with any real sex appeal, a short black dress.

So clichéd, she thought, critically assessing herself.

But it was the best thing she could come up with, short of driving into Lander and going to the mall.

Something she refused to do, as she'd already spent way too much time thinking about her date with Shilah tonight.

As she surveyed her image in the mirror, she thought about yesterday, when Shilah had surprised her by showing up at her father's clinic.

"Hey, you, thought I might find you here."

Ellie turned at the sound of Shilah's deep voice, surprised, believing she was alone in the clinic.

As she turned, rising from her chair, her knee chose that moment to knot and her ankle turned. She hissed in pain and would have fallen dead on her face had Shilah not rushed forward and gently cupped her beneath the elbow, steadying her.

"Careful, Ellie… A broken foot doesn't really figure into the plans I have for us," he said, and Ellie's glance flew to his.

"Plans? Am I missing something?" she asked. Despite her nonchalant reply, excitement rushed over her.

After a full week of work, she'd completed her investigation of the animals, the last of the blood drawn, labeled and carefully sent to the lab in Cheyenne. All that she had left was to wait for the results. Coupled with her final report as soon as the results were in, she'd be able to clear the ranch.

"I believe you finished the investigation?" he murmured, and she licked the full bottom rim of her mouth. Although she hadn't told him, she knew that he, like the rest of the ranch, knew she'd finished. She nodded her head, answering, "I have."

"Then I believe we have some business to take care of?" he murmured.

"We…we do?" she said, her voice barely above a whisper.

The edge of his sensual mouth curved, just the smallest bit.

Ellie drew in a swift breath.

"Yeah…we do," he said, and lowered his mouth, slanting it over hers.

With a sigh, she wrapped her arms around his neck, returning his kiss.

After giving her a deep, long kiss, suckling and caressing her mouth with his, until she cried out, her body pressing into his, he finally released her.

Ellie sank back down on her desk, her eyes dazed. He stroked a long finger down the side of her face, his gaze on her passion-swollen lips.

"I'll pick you up tonight at eight," he said, his tone slightly gruff, telling her he was as effected by the short exchange as she.

Without another word he turned and strode from the office, leaving a shaky Ellie with her fingers on her lips and an unknown smile on her face.

"Ellie?"

Ellie's glance flew to the mirror, to see her mother's image behind her, bringing her mind back to the present. She quickly gathered her scattered wits and turned to look at her mother, over her shoulder.

"What? Too short…too bland?" she asked, biting the corner of her mouth.

"No, I love the dress, pooh," she said, and Ellie

smiled lightly at the affectionate nickname her mother had called her from the time she was a child.

"And you're absolutely stunning in it," Leandra complimented, but the thoughtful expression remained on her face.

Ellie sighed. "Okay, Mom…so what's wrong with it?"

"It's just missing a certain…hmm. I don't know, baby…a little sexy sexy, maybe?" she asked, tilting her head to the side as she ran a critical gaze over Ellie.

Her mother's comment brought a sputtering laugh from Ellie. "A *what?* Sexy sexy… Mom, what are you talking about?"

Leandra moved in front of Ellie, unbuttoned the three pearl buttons on the dress, and to Ellie's surprise…and embarrassment, reached inside her dress to deftly adjust her bra straps before moving away.

A wicked grin curled the ends of Leandra's lips, "Now, *that's* sexy," she said clucking her tongue against the roof of her mouth.

"Mom…what are you doing? I can't go out like this!" Ellie's hands flew to her bra and her mother tapped the back of her wrists, hard, surprising a yelp from Ellie.

"And why not?"

Ellie blushed, slowly allowing her hands to fall to her sides, looking at herself in the mirror.

The adjustment, although minor, had given her cleavage a serious boost and the tops of her breasts swelled, barely contained behind her bra.

"My girls are too…out there."

This time it was Leandra who laughed. "And what is wrong with that? If you've got it…flaunt it. Nothing wrong with that at all. Your daddy never complains when I do," she said, smugly, and again a wicked grin split across her face. Ellie looked at her mother in open-mouthed surprise.

"Mom, please…I do not want to even *think* about Daddy liking your…"

"My sexy?" she said, laughing, obviously enjoying Ellie's discomfort. "We might be getting up there in age, baby, but that doesn't mean we don't—"

"Mom!" Although she didn't want to think of her parents in that way, Ellie's lips quirked at her mother's antics, grateful that she'd managed to, at least for the moment, helped to relieve the nervous knot in her stomach about her date with Shilah.

Leandra leaned over and planted a kiss on her cheek.

"You look beautiful, baby. Stop fretting so," she said, simply. "And Shilah is a lucky man to have someone like you."

At that, Ellie's glance flew to meet her mother's in the mirror. "It's—it's only a date, Mom."

Her mother stared at her, a grin quirking the side of her mouth.

Ellie frowned. "What's that look for?"

Leandra sighed deeply. "Baby, you've been in love with that boy since you were a young girl. And he's been just as crazy about you. I think it's more than just 'a date,'" she said, her answer shocking Ellie.

"What? You don't think I knew? I'm your mother, baby. Nothing gets past a mommy bear's watchful eyes," she said, laughing.

Ellie bit down on her bottom lip. "I don't know, Mom. He could have his pick of women. I'm just—"

"But you're the one he's chosen," Leandra cut in.

"And although I love him like he was my own—I love all the boys—in my opinion *he's* the one that got the best end of the bargain," she said, in motherly righteous indignation, as only a mother would, tugging a grin from Ellie.

"Thanks, Mom," she said, smiling at her mother's reflection in the mirror.

"Is this a mother-daughter-only moment, or are fathers allowed in the party?"

"Of course you are," Ellie said.

Her father strode into the room, to stand near her mother, wrapping his arms around her shoulders as the two of them watched Ellie as she sat on the bed and put her heels on.

Ellie began to feel like a bug under a microscope beneath her parents' admiring gazes…or better yet, she felt like a teenager again, going out on her first date.

Her mother must have read the expression on her face.

"Baby, why don't we leave El to finish getting ready by herself…besides, I have this new…dress…I want to show you, that I bought yesterday."

At that, Ellie caught what could only be termed a wicked gleam enter her father's eye. As he hustled her mother out of the room, Leandra gave Ellie a wink and blew her a kiss, leaving Ellie to stare after them with her mouth wide-open.

Ever since their getaway weeks ago, the one she'd suggested, her parents had been…acting like kids. Often Ellie would find them exchanging small kisses when they thought she wasn't around, and more than once her father had not so subtly asked her what time she'd be returning home. When she questioned him, his dark face would flush with color and he'd mumble that he and her mother wanted to make sure they were home when she got there.

But, Ellie hadn't bought it. She shook her head, the smile dipping away from her face.

Which brought another thought. As her investigation was ending, she had to make a decision, whether to stay in Lander and join her father, or return to her teaching position at the university.

Either way, she knew that she would have to find a place to stay. Not that her parents didn't want her— she knew they'd be more than happy for her to return home.

But her father would retire soon. And with that, her parents deserved time alone, something she realized more and more, since their return from their weekend in Cheyenne.

And then there was the question of Shilah and what would happen to them, now that she'd come to the end of the investigation.

Although she had no doubts the animals were clean of disease, there was still a fair amount of tension and anxiety on her part. What if by some outside chance some of the cattle were infected—what would that mean for her and Shilah and any hope they could ever have of having a relationship.

No matter what assurances he'd given her that he was able to separate what she had to do for her job from their personal relationship, doubts lingered. The what-if game played round and round in her mind, like an old-fashioned turntable, if the results were unfavorable.

Ellie contemplated the decisions facing her, as she put the finishing touches on her makeup.

* * *

Shilah was never nervous when it came to women. Never. He, like his brothers, had grown up with his fair share of dealings with the opposite sex. Truth be told, they all had more than their fair share.

Which is why he didn't understand what the hell it was about Ellie that seemed to put him in a constant state of nerves, the kind he'd had when he was a kid learning the ropes at the ranch, nervous and uncertain of his ability to perform.

Not since puberty had any woman had the ability to give him the type of knot in his gut he had whenever he was around Ellie.

He toyed with the neck of his beer bottle. The last week had been hell for him, having to keep his feelings to himself, not able to openly talk to her, for fear of what someone would see…interpret, if he did.

Hiding the way he felt, not only from everyone else, but from Ellie as well, afraid he'd scare her back into that damn shell of hers, that barrier she'd erected between herself and the world, one he was just as determined to break through.

But, for her, he'd stepped back, given her breathing room…the space she needed. As if she were a wild stallion, he had been…"gentling" her. Getting her used to the idea of them together, as a couple.

Yes, he knew there was truth to what she said, and neither did he want there to be any rumors of favoritism, knowing that the ranch's reputation was on the line. But now he was free. Free to show her how he felt, free to pick up where they'd left off and take their relationship to that place he wanted.

So why the hell was he sitting at home drinking,

alone, his gut tied in knots, when he was supposed to be picking her up in less than an hour.

He bit out a curse, and grabbed the bottle by the neck. Tilting his head back, he allowed the cold liquid to fill his mouth. He swirled the contents inside his mouth before taking a swallow.

A hard thump on his back almost made the beer come back up.

He spun around, a deep scowl on his face, as Nate plopped down next to him.

"Damn, man…you almost made me choke," he said, once he'd swallowed.

"Bad habit you have, with that. Been doing it since we were kids."

As though that was enough of an explanation he went on, "What are you doing home, anyway? I thought you had…plans."

Shilah slid a glance over at his brother, without answering. Lifting the beer he took his time, again swirling the contents in his mouth, his look warning Nate what he'd do to him if he repeated his action.

A half grin lifted Nate's face, and he raised his hands, silently promising not to repeat his offense.

"What are *you* doing home?" Shilah asked, turning the question back to his brother. "Don't you and Althea have plans?"

"Yeah, later on tonight. She wants to go check out that new Tyler Perry movie," he said, and Shilah openly smirked at him. "The things a man will do for the woman he loves know no boundaries," Nate replied with a shrug, before pushing off the stool and heading over to the refrigerator. "Mind if I join you?"

"Suit yourself," Shilah said with a shrug.

After Nate returned, he sat down next to Shilah again. "So...wanna tell me what the hell is going on with you and why you are at home, in the dark, nursing a beer alone, instead of being with Ellie?" he asked, surprising Shilah.

Nate barked out a laugh. "Uh...yeah, I know about you and Ellie."

"How? Shit," Shilah cursed, his response telling. "Does everybody know?"

"No. At least not that I know of. I know because you're my brother, and I know you. And I knew you wouldn't listen to a damn word I said when I warned you not to get involved with her," he said, reminding Shilah of the moment he'd taken him aside, when Ellie had first arrived on the ranch, and warned him away from her.

"Look, I stayed away from her. We both decided to cool off until after the investigation," Shilah responded, feeling a moment of guilt for his actions.

Nate lifted a brow. "Both of you decided?"

"Well...Ellie wouldn't have it any other way," he admitted, sheepishly. "Said she didn't want to compromise the results, have anyone thinking there was favoritism going on."

Nate nodded his head in approval. "Smart woman."

The two men drank in silence for long moments before Nate finished his beer and stood, facing Shilah.

"So, now that you're free to see each other, I'll ask you again.... What the hell are you doing at home?"

The question was simple and to the point. And one that brought a smile to Shilah's face.

He rose, finished the remnants of his beer and turned to head toward his suite. Before he left the room he turned back to his brother.

"Enjoy your movie, girlfriend," he said, his voice pitched unnaturally high, and laughed at his brother's single-finger salute.

Chapter 19

When they arrived at the restaurant, Ellie was a mass of nerves, her stomach knotting so badly she wished to God she'd thought to pack a bottle of the pink stuff in her purse.

When he'd picked her up at her parents, she'd been pleasantly surprised to see Shilah dressed to the nines, in casual dark slacks that molded and framed his long legs and thick thighs to perfection and a tailored white shirt, where she'd seen a sprinkling of dark hair at the open V-neck peek through. Although casual, the clothes fit his body as though they'd been tailor-made for him. She'd always known he was sinfully gorgeous, but tonight he gave an all new meaning to the word *fine*.

Afraid he'd catch her openly gawking at him, she averted her eyes.

After an awkward attempt at conversation she'd been ready to just give up, when he'd glanced over at her.

"You know, if that waiter looks at you one more time like you're something on the menu, I'm going to knock his teeth down his throat."

Her eyes flew to his, growing wide. "Shilah!"

"What? I saw him checking you out," he said, completely straight-faced.

She giggled, despite herself. "Shilah, that man is gay. He ain't *even* looking at me. Maybe you're the catch of the day he's dreaming about, for his own personal menu," she quipped, laughing harder at the way she turned the tables and the blush that crossed his face.

He scowled as she laughed. "Oh, you got jokes, huh?" Yet she saw the humor that darkened his eyes.

When the waiter returned to the table, Ellie could barely look at the man as she gave her order. He turned to Shilah and took his order, the wattage on the server's smile so bright it could have lit the entire restaurant. He'd barely left before Ellie was again laughing.

By the time their food arrived, the earlier tension was a thing of the past, and as they ate, their topics of conversation ranged from the latest in cattle to sports.

"Yeah, well, your precious Patriots are going down."

Ellie rolled her eyes. "Whatever. Not if the Jets' quarterback can't figure out how to dissect their cover two defense."

She laughed lightly at the look on his face. "What? Does it surprise you that I like football?" she asked, lifting a brow.

One side of his mouth hitched in a slow grin as he slid a wicked glance over her.

"Nothing about you surprises me, Ellie. You're a woman of many, *many* talents," he said, and Ellie felt an answering warmth rush over her body, forcing her to clench her thighs together in response.

"You're a bad, *bad* boy, Shilah Wilde…has anyone ever told you that?"

He looked away for a moment, the smile easing from his face. "Yeah, I've been told that a time or two."

Immediately the smile slipped from Ellie's face. She reached over and grasped his hand in hers. "Hey…I was just kidding."

He shook his head, saying, "Baby, I know. You're one of the few people who sees the good in me."

Ellie frowned, wondering where that came from. "Shilah?" When he drew her hand over, kissing the palm, her frown increased. She refused to allow him to brush it off and not answer her. He had dug enough at her, forced her to admit things to him, disclose things to him she never had to another person.

It was time to turn the tables.

"Hey, I'm serious, where did that come from?"

A flat look entered his eyes, and he allowed her hand to drop. "Just forget it, Ellie," he said, his expression closed up. Ellie blew out a breath of frustration.

"Fine. Forget I asked."

She stared down at her plate, pushing her food around, and for long moments there was nothing but silence. But this time it wasn't the easy one of moments before.

When the waiter returned to their table, she nodded her head, allowing him to remove her plate. He quickly returned with the cheesecake they'd ordered, but Ellie had lost her appetite for the dessert.

At that moment, music began to play, and she turned her head toward the miniuscule dance floor set up on the other side of the room. She reached for her glass of wine, watching couples make their way toward the dance floor.

She heard Shilah sigh, before his hands came out to remove her glass from her hands.

"You know a lot about me, Ellie. I've never kept anything from you. At least nothing important," he stated, quietly.

She lifted her eyes to look at him across the table, remaining silent.

He sighed. "Okay, shoot. What do you wanna know about me, woman? My life is an open book to you. My thoughts, emotions, feelings…whatever you want to know. Just ask."

She tilted her head to the side, considering him. "Open book, huh?" she asked, rubbing her hands together. "Ooo-hoo…let me see, so many questions, so little time!" she said, to which he uttered a heartfelt groan.

"Okay, okay. Seriously. Let's see…how about, where were you born? Besides Nate and Holt, do you have any other siblings, natural siblings? Are your parents still alive? Who—"

"Hey, one question at a time!" He laughed, but Ellie heard a nervous edge creep into his tone.

"I was born in Washington State, moved to Oregon, then Cali, and after that Idaho." He frowned. "No, after California it was Utah, and *then* Idaho. I think after Idaho we headed to Nevada—"

"Wait…haven't you lived in Wyoming from the time you were a child? I mean, I assumed…"

He shrugged, but despite his nonchalant expression, she caught a fleeting look cross his face, too fast for her to catalog the meaning, but enough that she read his discomfort…almost embarrassment, before it quickly left.

"I traveled with my mother's brother from the time I was around four or so, for about eight years, until we landed in Wyoming."

"You were raised by your uncle?"

"Guess you could say that," he replied, uttering a short laugh. "Sometimes I felt like I was raising him."

He raised his glass to his lips and took a drink, before continuing. "Look, Ellie, there's something I think you should know about me. Before I came to the ranch I used to hustle with my uncle."

"Hustle? What do you mean…."

"Look, my parents cut out on me before I even took my first steps, and had it not been for my uncle taking me in, well, I would have ended up on the streets or in foster care a lot earlier than I was. We lived on a reservation in New Mexico. Didn't have a lot of money in my family…my tribe. We lived on one of the poorer reservations. Money…resources were tight." He turned away briefly. "I don't want you to think less of me, Ellie. Your opinion means more to me than the air I breathe."

Ellie drew in a shuddered breath, reading the wealth of emotion in his eyes.

She knew that whatever Shilah was about to share with her wasn't something that was easy for him to talk about.

It probably wasn't something he even wanted to think about, if his set expression and the way he held his body stiff, tension rolling off of his wide shoulders, was any indication.

She placed her hand over his. Going on instinct, she

lifted it, brought it to her lips and placed a gentle kiss in the palm.

"There's nothing you can say that would make me think less of you, Shilah. Nothing," she said softly.

He closed his eyes briefly.

"My uncle and I moved around a lot. Ran every scam known, hustled any and everybody, he didn't care. As long as the money was good, there wasn't anything he wouldn't do to find a way to get it. He was good-looking, mostly used the way he looked on women." He stopped and shook his head. "Divorced, married, single, old and young, he didn't care. They were all fair game."

Quietly Ellie listened as he told her how as his uncle grew older, he'd brought Shilah into the game along with him.

"Finally he got caught by the feds. He got involved in a Medicare scam," he said. "He didn't know, but they'd been tracking him for a while, and set up a sting. He got busted, and I got sent to juvy and then to the boys' home. You know the rest," he said. Although he spoke matter-of-factly, Ellie read the shame in his eyes.

Ellie was quiet, digesting the information before she spoke. "Shilah, none of that was your fault," she finally said.

"I was more than willing to go along with it, Ellie. Yeah, I was a kid, but I could have said something… told someone what he was doing. I knew the score, but I kept silent. I helped him scam hundreds of people, Ellie. But he was family. The only family I had."

"Shilah, you were a child. There wasn't anything you could have done about what he was doing!"

He was shaking his head as she spoke. "I didn't have to go along with it, El. I knew right from wrong."

"Listen. I get that. But right or wrong, like you said, he was family. The only family you had. And you were a child, baby."

At her words, he swung his head around, staring at her so intently she grew uncomfortable.

"What?"

A slow smile crossed his sensual lips. "That's the first time you've called me that."

She frowned, thinking, and blushed when she realized what she'd called him. She'd never called a man *baby* before. As silly as it would probably sound if she confessed that aloud, the fact that she had called him *baby* brought a blush to her face.

"Well, yeah. Guess I did," she said, and they stared across the table at each other, both with grins on their faces. Silly grins.

"And, *baby*," she said, elongated it to make him laugh. "Listen to me when I say you're one of the finest men I know. And I don't just mean the way you look," she said, wiggling her brows up and down, pulling a startled bark of laughter from Shilah.

"You're not that kid you were. And you have nothing to be ashamed of. Nothing."

He reached across the small table and brought their lips together.

"You're a special man, Shilah Wilde," she whispered against his mouth, before he claimed her lips.

When he released her, she sat back in her chair, and smiled across at him.

"So...what exciting thing is next for you, Ellie? Now that you know my life story. What about you? Now that the investigation is over, are you going to stick around for a while? Help your dad at his practice?" Although the change of topic was abrupt, Ellie felt none of the anger she'd felt before, when she'd felt he was holding back from her.

She lifted her glass of wine to her lips, stalling for time, as she thought of how to answer his question.

She shrugged. "I guess a lot of that depends," she said, after swallowing.

"Depends on what?" he asked, giving her that heart-stopping, nipple-beading smile of his that always made her insides turn straight to butter.

Taking a mental deep breath, she plunged in. "Depends on if I'm given another reason to stay."

Chapter 20

As soon as she said it, Ellie wished to God she could retract the words. The thoughtful look on his face made a deep flush creep along her skin.

God, what had she been thinking, she wondered. What had she been thinking by putting herself out there like that?

"Ellie, baby, I—"

Whatever he'd been about to say, the waiter interrupted to clear their plates, and Ellie was more than happy for the reprieve.

When the DJ put on one of Ellie's favorite songs, she bounced in her chair, placing fake enthusiasm into her voice, saying, "Ohh, I love this song!"

Shilah leaned back in his chair, a smile tugging the corners of his mouth. "Wanna give it a whirl?" he asked, nodding toward the dance floor.

"Oh God, no!" she said, her eyes flying to his.

Without a word, he rose and hauled her to her feet. He ignored her groaning protest and led her to the dance floor.

Doing her *best* to "shake what her mama gave her," as the song suggested, she giggled at Shilah as he danced along with her, grabbing her by the waist and twirling her around until she felt giddy. Breathless, she grinned up at him, the music and dancing easing away the tension.

When the music changed, the upbeat tempo of the last song ended and was replaced by a slower one. Ellie glanced up at Shilah, the laughter still in place.

"Where are you going? If I remember correctly, this used to be one of your favorite songs?" he both stated and asked.

"Yeah," she said, slightly out of breath from dancing. "It was. But after that, I don't think I have enough energy to keep on dancing—you wore me out!" She laughed.

"Don't worry, El...I have enough energy for the both of us." The smile eased from her mouth at the look in his piercing dark eyes, the hint of a smile that creased his lean cheeks.

"Dance with me, Ellie?" he asked, his voice dropping an octave and sending electric heat through her body.

One arm remained wrapped around her waist, the other moved lower, casually cupping her buttocks, bringing her flush against his long, hard frame.

As Shilah held her close, Ellie felt that nervous jitter return, the same one she'd felt at the beginning of the date, and took deep breaths, to quell her nervous anticipation. She had put it on the back burner, but now it returned to blazing life as they moved together, as one, in small swaying motions.

Their bodies moved together as though that's what they'd been created for. She loved everything about the evening, from the way he'd shared a piece of his past with her, to the sensuality of the song, the feel of his body and the way he moved her—it was all magic.

A magic that had been building for the last three weeks since she'd been home. A magic she didn't want to end.

She was made for him.

Shilah felt his heartbeat ricocheting around his chest as he held Ellie close.

After a few moments, he felt the tension leave her limbs and her body mold to his, as though they'd danced a thousand times together.

When he felt her head come to rest on his chest, he laid his head lightly against the top of her head, breathing in the scent of her shampoo. A light, sweet smell, mixed with her own womanly scent, one that was as uniquely intoxicating and beautiful as she herself.

Just like her, it was perfect.

When a particularly energetic couple bumped into them, he deftly moved her, pressing their bodies closer together, loving the way her slight curves felt against his body. As they danced their bodies moved together effortlessly, as one.

Although he'd been surprised at her earlier reticence, the fact that she was obviously nervous about their evening together had made Shilah realize that she was as excited about their being together as he.

It had been so easy to talk to her, easy to share things

with her that he hadn't shared with another. With Ellie, it seemed as though there wasn't anything he couldn't talk to her about, share with her.

He thought back to the look that had crossed her face when he'd asked her what her plans were after the investigation. His heart had crashed against his chest at her response. He'd been about to ask her if he would be reason enough for her to stay when the waiter's ill-timed arrival had prevented it.

Immediately he felt her embarrassment, her need to change the subject, and allowed her a reprieve. For the moment.

He'd hidden his grin, the knowledge that she cared for him as much as he did for her making his steps lighter as he led her to the dance floor.

Since her return home, she'd managed to carve an even deeper wedge in his heart than before. He wasn't ready for what they had…what they could have, to come to an end.

She shifted, her body sliding against his and, glancing down at her, he pulled away enough so that he could see her beautiful face.

Without thought to who was watching, or where they were, he cupped her face, leaned down and captured her full lips with his, hoping that in his kiss she knew the answer to her question.

He had no intention of allowing the magic of what they had to end, anytime soon.

After he released her, she stared up at him, her lids low, droopy, her mouth swollen from his kisses.

She placed her head on his chest, her hand over his heart, as they again moved as one to the searing lyrics.

* * *

As the song ended, Ellie reluctantly lifted her head from Shilah's chest, her body trembling.

When she would have pulled away, he moved her closer, lifting her hand, kissing the palm in the familiar caress, one that did all the right things for her.

He lowered his head and softly ran his nose against the curve of her cheek. The hand at her waist moved lower, until he lightly held her butt, bringing their bodies flush, and lightly grinding her against the steely length of his erection.

"I need you," he whispered, his voice deep, gruff with need.

A need that mirrored hers.

Ellie nodded her head, licking her tongue across lips gone dry.

"I—I just need to call home and let my folks know I'm not coming home tonight."

Her heart seemed to jump from her chest when she saw the wicked gleam enter his eyes, as he took her hand in his and led her away from the dance floor.

After paying the bill, they were leaving the restaurant when Ellie heard her cell phone ring. She would have ignored it, but the special ringtone she'd assigned to her parents had her digging inside her purse to pull the phone out.

With an apologetic shrug, she pressed the small indention on the phone and lifted it to her ear.

"Ellie, honey, I hate to disturb you, but I need you at the Wilde Ranch," her father said, and Ellie frowned.

"What is it, Dad? Is everything okay?"

Her father hastened to assure her that it was, but that

he needed her to help him in the unexpected twin birth of foals that was proving to be a difficult delivery.

"With this kind of birth, the boys usually are pretty well able to help, but all of them are out, and Jake took the weekend off to visit his folks," he said, mentioning the foreman. "Baby, I hate to ask you—"

"No, Dad, that's fine! I'm with Shilah now. We'll be there in twenty minutes," she said, and after a quick farewell ended the call.

"Dad needs me," she began, hoping he wouldn't be upset. But the strain in her father's voice and his need for her overrode anything else.

"I know. I heard. I can get us there in ten minutes," he said with a wink, and Ellie smiled at him gratefully as he ushered her out of the restaurant.

Chapter 21

"You look good wearing my robe."

Ellie turned around at the sound of Shilah's voice, grasping the lapels of his robe tighter around her body.

As promised, Shilah had cut the twenty-minute drive in half. As they'd arrived at the ranch, she'd quickly saddled up and ridden the short distance to where her father was in the difficult process of delivering the second of two breech-birth foals.

With Ellie's professional help, the second foal's birth had been less traumatic, and the delivery had gone much faster.

When she began helping her father with the cleanup, he stopped her, saying, "I think the boys can handle it from here. Why don't you go back to your date?" He cast her a knowing glance, which made her blush.

She'd stood up on tiptoe and kissed her father's cheek

and left, riding back to the house. When she'd arrived, she'd met up with Yasmine in the kitchen and was told that Shilah was out with his brothers, on an emergency.

Yasmine had nonchalantly suggested Ellie use Shilah's bathroom to clean up, looking at the blood and dirt covering her from head to toe.

She'd just finished bathing and, looking around for something to wear, had donned his robe.

"I'm a mess. I—I thought I'd take a quick shower before going home. The birth was pretty messy. I didn't think you were here. Dad mentioned that you and your brothers had an emergency of your own," Ellie said, knowing she was babbling, as doubt came over her. "I'll just get my clothes on and get out of here," she mumbled, gathering her ruined dress and shoes. His next words stopped her.

"You're beautiful."

Ellie suppressed the shiver that ran through her at the scalding-hot look in his eyes. Flustered, she turned away, clutching her dress in one hand and hooking the straps of her heels with the other.

"Is everything okay? I went by to check up on you and your dad. By the time I got there, your dad had already left. The guys told me everything went well."

"Yes, actually the birth went fairly fast after we got the first foal out. Both mama and babies are doing well."

As he advanced toward her, she took an involuntary step back, looking around the room.

"I'll just uh, go and get dressed and get out of your way. I'm sure you want to use the bathroom." She was so flustered she dropped her clothes, and as she bent to retrieve them, his hand covered hers.

"It's okay, I don't mind. In fact I kinda like you being here," he said, his eyes hooded as his glance slid over her.

"Why don't we take one, together?" he asked, and her eyes flew to his.

"Take one, what?" she asked, although she knew exactly what he was referring to. The thought of taking a bath with Shilah was as exciting as it was intimidating.

His wicked grin almost brought her to her knees. "Let me wash you, Ellie."

He pushed away from the wall, advancing toward her, stopping when he was less than a foot away from her.

"I, uh...already washed up. Anyway, I don't think that would be a good idea." She stuttered the words, backing up until her back was flush against the wall.

She had no problems with her body, and the scars on her knees were nothing more than reminders of what she'd survived. But the thought of bathing with him...of him washing her... She closed her eyes tight as though to force away the image of him doing something so intimate to her.

"Has anyone ever told you that you think too much?" he asked, his warm breath fanning the side of her face.

"Shilah..." she whispered.

Her breath escaped in a long hiss of pleasure when he continued to nuzzle her neck, licking a scalding path from beneath the lobe of her ear, down the side, his talented, wicked tongue finding the hollow of her throat to place an open-mouthed kiss.

She felt one of his big hands move aside his robe, and his hand, hot, hard, move inside the thick terry cloth and grasp her breast.

She moaned, her body arching when his other hand

reached down lower and moved back and forth over the springing hairs of her mound.

When his fingers found her clit, lightly pinching the nubbin until it beaded, filling with blood, Ellie's body arched sharply, her back pressing against the door as his fingers pressed inside her moist opening, deeper.

"Tell me you want me, Ellie. Tell me you need me." He breathed the demanding words against her face.

Ellie moved her head to the side, allowing his tongue to slide and glide over her throat, his teeth to nip and caress the hollow of her throat.

She shouldn't want him with a need that was growing out of control. One kiss. One touch…one look. That was all it took.

He slanted his mouth over hers, his tongue coming out to play and mate with hers, promising what he wanted their bodies to do.

When he pulled away, both of their breaths were ragged. He stared down at her with an intensity in his eyes that showed, vividly, his need.

A feeling that resonated deep inside Ellie. A need she never knew she'd had, until she'd come back home.

Since she'd returned to Shilah.

Instead of the thought frightening her, this overwhelming need she had for him, instead it felt…right.

He said nothing more, yet in his eyes she knew what he wanted her to say, what he was demanding she say, before he would end the ache inside her.

She closed her eyes and bowed her head, her mind, her emotions scattered.

She raised her head, meeting his gaze. In his gaze she saw uncertainty…and love. A love so strong it nearly staggered her in its intensity.

"I—I don't just want you, Shilah," she said, drawing in a deep breath before plunging in. "I—I love you." No sooner had the words escaped than he was lifting her in his arms, slashing his mouth over hers as he backed her against the wall, lifting her legs to straddle his waist.

"God…I love you too, Ellie." His voice shook with deep emotion as he pulled his mouth from hers, his busy hands gliding over her naked body, as he ran scalding kisses over her face.

Ellie moaned, softly his chest warm against her breasts, as he pressed her back into the cold wall, the steely length of his cock pressed against her vagina.

She hissed, her body bowing away from the wall when his hand moved down between their bodies, his knuckles pressing against her stomach as he fisted his shaft.

She hissed when she felt the tip of his shaft between her wet folds, rubbing back and forth between the seam of her lips.

"Tell me I'm the only man you want…that you'll ever want," he demanded, pressing the tip of his shaft, just the tip, inside her body.

"Yes…baby, yes, only you," she cried brokenly.

He grunted his satisfaction and in one long, sure stroked embedded deep inside her.

Ellie bit down on her lip harshly, drawing blood, squeezing her eyes tightly closed, her body tensing as he fed her his entire length.

Once fully inside he stopped, allowing her to grow accustomed to his length and girth.

"Are…are you okay?" he asked, his voice barely recognizable, his breathing harsh in the quiet room.

She licked her bottom lip, wiggling her body, trying to ease the sweet ache between her legs at his invasion.

"Keep that up and this will definitely be over too soon, baby," he groaned, his laugh harsh against the side of her neck. "And I want this to last."

She nodded her head, taking deep, even breaths, forcing her body to relax around his invasion.

Once he was assured she was okay, she felt his body move.

She loved him. The words reverberated around his head as Shilah moved inside her, fighting off the way the sweet feel of her warm, wet walls clenching and releasing his cock threatened to make his seed burst from him.

The knowledge that she loved him too washed over him like a much-needed rain after a drought. His hands roamed over her, refamiliarizing himself with her the perfect lines of her body, over her back, and the nipped-in indenture of her tiny waist, cupping the muscled contours of her perfect ass.

As he worked his body inside her, he heard her gasp as his finger darted along the seam of her butt, separating the round globes, as he plunged inside her, her body jostling as he moved in and out of her in short, powerful thrusts.

It wasn't enough. As he plunged and retreated inside her body, her cries echoing off the walls, he knew this feeling of being inside would never be enough.

Ellie bit down on her lip to prevent the scream she felt at the back of her throat threatening to erupt. As he thrust inside her, his strokes became hotter, harder, more demanding. Had his strong arms not held her pinned to the wall, she would have crumbled to the floor, unable to support her own weight.

Her legs, wrapped around him, quivered and her breath came out in choked gasps as he stroked inside her body.

Her head rolled back and forth against the wall, her body on fire. She tightened her hold around his neck, her nails scoring deep into his flesh. He barked out a completely masculine laugh but she didn't care.

No one had ever made love to her like this. No one had managed to tap deep inside her, pull out the responses, wild out-of-control responses, like Shilah.

"Baby…baby, I'm coming," she heard him roar, his voice sounding muffled against the roar in her own ears, as though from a distance.

He hoisted her higher on his shaft, his hand coming out to slap her butt, while he delivered one, two, three more corkscrew thrusts and she went over the edge.

Crystal-like shards of glass flashed behind her eyes as she felt her own orgasm rip through her body.

She gave in to the release, throwing her head back, her body no longer hers, she gave in, completely, mind, body and soul to Shilah.

After her mind-numbing release, she allowed her trembling legs to slide down his body. She'd have fallen had he not lifted her high in his arms, cradling her against his chest and carrying her to the bed.

She smiled, drowsy and content, as, moments after placing her on the bed, she felt the bed shift and his chest drape against her back.

His cock, still hard, rested against the curve of her back and he reached around to cup her mound. When she felt a thick finger move inside her body, she gasped.

"Shilah?" she asked, sleepily, her voice hoarse.

"I'm not done with you yet." His hot words whispered against her neck, brought her eyes wide open and her mouth form a perfect O.

Chapter 22

Early dawn light peaked through the wide-slatted blinds in Shilah's bedroom as Ellie lay close, tucked against his side, their bodies so close that nothing, not even the sheet he'd finally drawn over them after their marathon lovemaking, separated them.

Her head lay pillowed on his wide chest, while he had one arm draped around her waist, his long fingers caressing her bottom.

A sigh of hedonistic pleasure left her lips and a lazy smile tilted the corners of her mouth as she felt his deft hands stroking over her body, yet she kept her eyes closed.

She couldn't have lifted them even had she wanted to, their long night of lovemaking leaving her too weak to move even her eyes.

She felt the bed shift as he moved, and within seconds she was carefully maneuvered until she lay on her back.

Another slight movement, the sound of a drawer opening and the rip of foil, and she drew in a deep, long breath and waited, as expectancy gripped her.

At that moment someone knocked on the door.

"Ignore it, they'll go away." He mouthed the words against her mouth. But the insistent knocking grew, followed by the sound of Holt's voice, warning Shilah what would happen if he didn't answer the damn door and starting a countdown.

Shilah bit out a curse, and with a sigh and one last kiss, moved away from Ellie, his glance raking over her.

"He's on number three. You'd better answer the door before he gets to one," she said with a laugh.

Shilah gave her another swift kiss, bounded from the bed.

Before making it to one, Holt was opening the door, as Shilah stood bare naked in the center of the room.

"Aww, man...I don't wanna see that. Put some damn clothes on!" Holt put his hands out as though shielding himself from the view.

"Then don't walk into my room unannounced," Shilah grunted, grabbing his slacks from the floor and shoving them up his legs.

It was then Holt noticed Ellie and swiftly turned away. "Ohh...sorry, Ellie. I didn't know you were here! My bad."

"Yeah, your bad. Now get the hell out of here. I'll be out in a sec," Shilah said, turning to make sure Ellie had the sheet over her body.

Although embarrassed to be caught in Shilah's bed, Ellie giggled at the four different shades of red Holt had turned before hastily making his retreat.

Striding toward the door, Shilah turned, his hand on the knob. "Don't go anywhere. I'll be right back."

After he left, Ellie snuggled down deeper into the sheets. Her glance fell to the discarded condom, halfway out of the foil wrap, unused as they'd been interrupted.

A slow grin stretched across her lips. She had no plans to go anywhere anytime soon.

Ellie woke, stretching, and cracked open her eyes, quickly shutting them again as the sunlight beamed down on her from the skylight in Shilah's room.

"God...what time is it?" she groaned, yawning widely.

She turned her head toward the bedside table and the clock radio, its neon-blue lights indicating the hour.

It was just past nine a.m. She must have fallen asleep... but where was Shilah, she thought, frowning as she glanced around the room.

With a groan she lifted her torso from the bed, throwing her legs over the side, when her eyes lit on a note laid across Shilah's pillow.

With a frown, she lifted the small note and opened it, her eyes scanning over the bold letters, a blush stealing across her face as she read the succinct note.

Will be back soon to pick up where we left off...

She shook her head, rising from the bed. The man had the sexual energy of a randy stallion, she thought, wincing as her legs trembled when she stood.

She inhaled a long, shaky breath.

Her thighs, back, between her legs, even her breasts, all had the same sweet ache that forced her to place a hand out on the bed to steady herself.

Strike that; the man made a stallion look like the newborn foals she'd helped her father deliver yesterday, she thought, and she gingerly walked to the end of the bed. She grabbed the towel they'd used last night and wrapped it around her body.

Deciding a long hot shower was exactly what the doctor ordered, she turned toward the bathroom. Halfway there, she remembered a small bottle of her favorite lotion was in her purse and walked toward the door to retrieve it.

As she lifted the purse from where it sat near the door, she frowned, seeing a large manila envelope had been pushed under the door.

A half grin crossed her face, as she saw her name written across the top, wondering what Shilah had placed inside for her.

She slid her finger beneath the seal and lifted out the contents, frowning as she held in her hand what appeared to be printouts of images.

Moving toward the light to see the pictures better, she stopped, a strangled gasp escaping from her throat.

Nausea burned in her stomach and she sank to the bed, staring in horrified numbness at the images.

Photos of she and Shilah, together; from the first time he'd taken her to lunch, his arm loosely wrapped around her waist, casually, to the night he'd shown up at her father's clinic to ask her out…to late last night when they had lain, their bodies intertwined after making love.

The pictures dropped from her nerveless hands to cascade to the bed.

Nausea swelled, filling her gut, when she spied a note that had been included with the pictures.

Ellie hesitated, not sure she wanted to read the contents. With trembling hands she lifted the note, reading it.

For you, Shilah.

The knot of nausea grew and, stumbling from the bed, she ran to the bathroom, barely making it to the toilet before her stomach emptied.

Chapter 23

Although exhausted from helping his brothers clean up the mess and re-capture the cattle that had gotten free from one of the new pastures, Shilah was bounding up the stairs, two at a time, rushing to return to Ellie.

The entire time he'd been helping his brothers, his mind had been on Ellie, their night together. The memory of how well she fit him, both in and out of bed, had been on his mind throughout the morning.

It had been a long time since he'd felt as he did; happy, content…he laughed out loud. Hell, he'd never felt like this before. But, she brought the joy out in him. Made him believe that he was worthy of love. And knowing she loved him as well had sealed it for him.

He was going to do it; he was going to ask Ellie to marry him. There was no one else he wanted, no one else made him feel the way she did. He knew no other ever would.

He'd wrestled with the thought as he'd helped his brothers, distracted, a part of him afraid of her answer, although she'd told him she loved him.

She said she loved him, but did she love him enough to take a chance on him? Take a chance on them, and bind herself to him, for the rest of her life?

She valued her independence, a hard-fought independence. One he knew had come from a steely determination to overcome the curve life had thrown her at a young age.

If it took her a little while longer to come to the same conclusion he had, that she wanted to spend the rest of her life with him, as he did with her, he was willing to wait.

He'd wait as long as necessary.

Taking a fortifying breath, he opened the door to his room and walked inside. When he saw her standing in front of the single, large window, staring out, he walked over to her. Leaning down, he placed a kiss on the side of her neck.

"Hey, baby, I'm sorry that took so long. I—"

The minute she turned around, his heart seemed to stop beating for a moment at the look in her red-rimmed eyes.

"Baby, what's wrong?"

When she simply stared up at him, her large doe-shaped eyes rimmed in red, he ran his hands over her, glancing down at her knee, his first thought that she'd somehow hurt herself.

When she said nothing, he frowned. "Are your parents okay?" Again, she said nothing. He looked closely at her, saw the anger behind the tears, the set cast of her features, and his gut hollowed out.

"You're scaring me, Ellie. Wha—"

She turned away from him. Calmly walking over to the bed, she lifted a large yellow envelope in her hand and turned back to face him.

"I think this was meant for you."

Shilah's glance ran from her set face, back to the envelope she held in her hand.

Slowly he walked toward her, taking the envelope. He lifted the flap and drew out the contents.

The minute he saw what was inside, a fury unlike anything he'd ever felt gripped him as he leafed through the pictures.

"Where did you get this?" he bit out.

"They were left under your door. Guess whoever put them there didn't think I'd still be around," she said, laughing humorlessly.

"What's that supposed to mean, El?" he asked, reaching out to touch her.

She jerked back, her nostrils flaring, anger rolling off her slim frame. "Don't call me that," she said, and he allowed his hands to drop to his sides.

"Obviously you didn't take the pictures." She laughed harshly. "You left that up to someone else. Be kinda hard to take these types of pictures yourself," she said, her laugh shrill, unnatural. "I've got to hand it to you, Shilah. When you said family meant everything to you—" she stopped, shaking her head "—you meant it."

His glance flew to hers, his eyes narrowing even more at the hint of accusation. "Surely you don't think I had anything to do with this, El…Ellie?" he asked, a new type of anger replacing the one at seeing the pictures.

She spun around, facing him. "What am I supposed to think, Shilah?" she asked, her voice no longer flat, her eyes blazing…accusing.

"You're supposed to think that someone else did this. Not me."

"Why? Who would have anything to gain by that? No," she said. "Do you want me to tell you what I think?"

He crossed his arms across his chest. "Yes, why don't you tell me?" he asked, flatly.

"I think you knew about this. In fact—" She stopped, her eyes narrowing. "Maybe you and your brothers were afraid of what the investigation would show and thought you'd stack the odds in your favor, just in case."

She laughed, shaking her head. "Sad thing is I was just going to tell you today that the results came back last night. Preliminary, but they cleared the ranch." She shook her head, choking down tears. "None of this was necessary. The ranch was going to be cleared."

Shilah waited for her to continue, remaining silent. If he said anything now, he knew he'd regret it. The very fact that she believed he and his brothers would use her like this, was like a knife. He felt the pain of her doubt and accusations pierce his skin and rip through his heart.

He turned away from her, unable to look at her face.

To think he'd wanted to ask her to marry him, to become a part of his family, a family she thought capable of something so horrendous.

"You didn't have to screw the cripple after all."

At her words, the knife drove the rest of the way through his heart. He turned away from her.

"Get out."

When she said nothing more, he kept his back to her and repeated the demand.

"Get the hell out and don't ever show your face at my home again."

Chapter 24

"So this is where my mad scientist is holed up. Thought I might find you here."

Ellie spun around in her chair and with a tired smile glanced at her father standing in the doorway.

"What are you still doing here, Dad? Thought you'd left hours ago," she asked, watching as he strode inside.

"Naw, thought I'd hang around for a little longer. Your mama is having that bongo game of hers tonight with some women from her church group."

Ellie laughed. "That would be bunko, Dad," she said, correcting her father.

"Craps, that's what it really is. And to think these are supposedly upstanding women in the community... No shame," he said, shaking his head. But Ellie saw the twinkle in his eyes and knew that her father was trying his best to make her smile, something she hadn't done… hadn't felt like doing, since her breakup with Shilah.

"These women have no shame."

"Dad, come on, it's just a harmless game!"

"With dice," he said, lifting a brow. "Where they play for money." He shook his head again. "I don't know, El, sounds like craps to me."

Ellie burst out laughing and her father grinned at her. When her laughter subsided he came to stand next to her, running his hand over her hair.

"Good to see you smile, baby girl." He frowned, running a critical glance over her. "You look tired. Can't you wrap this up for the night? Maybe those hustlers left us something to eat. I think they should be leaving soon," he said, referring again to her mother's friends, tugging another smile from Ellie.

With a sigh she spun back around.

"Can't. I—I have to finish this," she said, and turned back to the clutter on her desk, sifting through it to find the file she was looking for.

From the corner of her eye she saw her father discreetly move his glance away from the screen of her laptop, where her typed notes were in plain view.

She turned to her father, unknowingly biting the corner of her lips.

"What's wrong, Ellie? I can tell something is bothering you. And before you say it—" He raised a finger, before she could make the automatic response. "Yes, I know you can't tell me details. I wouldn't ask that of you. But, if I can help in any small way, you know you can trust me, El."

Ellie sighed. "I know that, Dad. And it's not that I don't trust you." She shook her head, laughing humorlessly.

"Besides, it's not as though I need to worry about any taint to the investigation." She drew in a shuddering breath, tears of frustration and loss clouding her eyes as she looked up at her father. "Been there, done that."

Seeing the concern in his eyes, she turned away, wiping the corner of her eyes with the back of her hand.

"Ellie," he murmured, "is there anything I can do? Why don't you let me talk to Shilah," he said, and she broke away, shaking her head vehemently.

"No, Dad. Please, just leave it."

After giving her a considering look he slowly nodded his head, deferring to her.

"I think I've already messed up enough," she said. "He doesn't want to see me or talk to me. And I don't want to get you involved with this. I'm a big girl." She forced a smile on her lips. "I can take care of myself,"

"Yeah, but you're always going to be my baby girl." He sat down in the chair next to her, sighing heavily. "Doesn't stop me from worrying about you. Never will," he finished gruffly. Again, her father brought a reluctant laugh to her lips.

"And I wouldn't have you any other way," she said, a small smile on her face as she glanced at her father.

Tired lines bracketed his face, and she felt a moment of guilt, knowing she was the reason.

For the last week both her father and mother had been worrying over her, since she'd been fired from the project.

And, although she hadn't told them—not yet ready to talk about it, still sorting through the range of emotions, from pain and loss to betrayal—she knew they were also aware of her breakup with Shilah.

After wrestling with the decision about what to do about the photos, she'd come to the conclusion that simply because they existed, no matter who had taken them, she had no choice but to tell Clarence, her supervisor at Jasper and Brant.

When she'd made the call, afraid of what his reaction would be, she'd haltingly related the trail of events, and despite the shame, she admitted that she had entered into a relationship with Shilah Wilde. She'd continued, telling him of the pictures, how she'd found them and where.

There'd been a long moment of silence before Clarence had spoken. Afraid of his reaction, she'd been rendered speechless at his response.

Ethically, he had no choice but to pull her from the investigation and bring in another investigator. But he wouldn't disclose the true reasons to anyone, least of all the USDA, not wanting to ruin Ellie's reputation.

She'd closed her eyes, emotion overcoming her. She'd informed him that she believed the ranch was innocent of the charges, based on the blood work and her own observations. She had offered to pass the final report on to him so that he could give it to the new investigator. He'd quickly rejected her offer, his voice gentle, telling her that although he wouldn't disclose what she'd done, he had no choice but to begin the investigation all over.

When she'd asked what that meant for the Wilde Ranch, he'd told her, regret in his voice, that it likely meant quarantine, due to time constraints. At her gasp, he quickly went on to say it would be only temporary.

"I'm fine." Her shoulders slumped. "It's just that now I don't know what this will mean for the ranch. God, I feel so awful," she said, her voice breaking. "And there's nothing I can do about it. Until this is all cleared up... Dad, they could lose everything," she said, tears burning her eyes.

"Ellie, this isn't your fault, and there isn't a thing you can do. I won't lie and say this isn't serious, damn serious," he said, his face and tone grim. "But they'll get through this. They're a strong family. They've been through a lot."

She nodded her head, swallowing the pain in her heart as Shilah's face, bland, neutral as she had flung her accusations at him as he'd faced her, flashed in her mind. She hung her head down low, remembering the look of pain she'd seen in his dark eyes before he'd turned away from her and ordered her off his property.

Piggybacking that memory was the one of Shilah holding her close after they'd made love and sharing a part of his life with her...trusting her enough to share things he'd never shared with another, even the men he called brothers.

The flare of emotion in his beautiful eyes when he'd called her family.

She turned her face away from her dad, not wanting him to see the emotion she knew she was unable to hide from him.

She'd compromised her professional integrity and risked her license, the threat of which still loomed ominously over her head like a black cloud. But what hurt more than anything was the knowledge that Shilah had been playing with her, toying with her feelings, pretending to care for her as desperately as she had fallen for him.

He hadn't even bothered denying the accusations.

She hardened her heart.

"God, how could I have been so stupid?"

Her father gathered her in his arms, and for long moments simply hugged her. "Baby girl, when it comes to love, there is no such thing as stupid," he said, his expression thoughtful.

"I'm proud of you, Ellie. I always have been. And no matter what *anyone* says, I know that you are a woman of integrity. I know you wouldn't…didn't…allow your relationship with Shilah to influence you one way or another. And when they bring that new investigator in, and they find out the same thing you did, not only will the boys be exonerated, so will you."

At his words, the small control she had broke away and she let the tears fall, crying silently as she allowed her father to hold her tight in his arms. "Thank you, Dad," she whispered against his chest.

When she felt in better control, she pulled away and silently accepted the tissue he offered.

"Guess I'd better get back to work, Dad. Gotta clear all this up, send in my final report," she said. Although Clarence had told her he wouldn't need her report, Ellie wanted to complete the job, if for no other reason than her own professional satisfaction.

With a nod, her father leaned down and kissed the side of her head.

"Baby girl, no matter what, remember what I said." Ellie smiled a tremulous smile and slowly he turned and left.

Ellie gathered the remaining documents, carefully placing them in the file folder and turned to retrieve her disk, the one she'd backed up with all of her information from the investigation.

Her professional dignity was about all she had right now, and no matter what, she was going to finish the job. It was all she had right now.

If she could just convince Clarence to submit her report, maybe she'd be able to salvage some of her dignity, knowing findings would be under tight scrutiny. *Any* chance she had of saving face...including her reputation, rested on her report.

She sat back in her chair, and blindly reached for her coffee, bringing it to her lips and grimacing as the now cold liquid slid down her throat.

She glanced over at the clock, and noting the time, knew that despite the lateness of the hour, she wouldn't be going to bed anytime soon.

Between losing her job and losing Shilah, sleep was definitely not in the cards for her tonight, any more so than it had been for the last few days.

A frown marred her forehead as she thought over her last conversation with Clarence. At the time they'd spoken, she'd been so grateful when he'd said he wouldn't disclose the reason she was leaving the investigation, she'd nearly wept in relief. Now she thought of the conversation and his avowals of believing that despite her relationship with Shilah she had no bias. He had declined her offer to submit her report.

She fully understood why he felt ethically bound to remove her, but why not accept her report? The question nagged at Ellie long after she'd left the clinic and as she lay in bed that night, eyes closed, yet sleep elusive. There was something about the complete faith he claimed to have in her that didn't jive with his refusal to accept her report.

Why do that, unless...

Her eyes sprang open and her stomach felt as though it dropped to her knees, as a thought came to her mind of another reason he would have for getting her out of the picture.

She knew what she had to do, the only thing she could do, if for no other reason than she was damned if she'd let anyone set her up and blackmail her, covertly or not.

And that was exactly what Clarence had done.

Chapter 25

Although she'd made the three-hour drive to Cheyenne by noon, at 7:00 p.m. Ellie was just pulling into the parking lot of the building that housed the executive offices of Jasper and Brant. A glance around the lot showed it to be as deserted as she'd hoped.

With her stomach tied in knots, Ellie cut the engine on her car and sat with her hands clenching the wheel so tight her knuckles strained.

She relaxed her grip and took a deep, calming breath. During the last week, time after time she'd found herself lifting her cell to punch in her supervisor's number, only to lose her nerve and press the end button before the call could go through.

At first she had thought it was nerves holding her back, or the lack of courage in confronting the man. She had wondered if it was all in her mind, not wanting to accuse him of something so low.

And then she'd remembered in shame how she'd accused the man she claimed to love of the low act.

Throughout the long drive, she'd thought over everything that had happened, from her being fired to the ugly accusations she'd thrown at Shilah.

What kept cropping up in her mind was the careful way he'd held his body, the almost neutral expression on his face. But it was his eyes that had told a different story. His eyes held a different truth, one that in her hurt and anger…confusion, she hadn't seen.

She'd made the decision to come to the office and confront him face-to-face. As she made the long drive, a different plan began to hatch in her mind instead, and so after her arrival, she waited until long after she thought he'd left for the day before making her way to Jasper and Brant.

With a heavy sigh retrieved her bag and left the car. Glancing around the nearly empty parking lot, Ellie hoped that she hadn't made the drive unnecessarily and that Clarence was still in his office.

She walked to the entry of the building, and peering into the large glass double doors, saw a guard nearby.

She flashed her badge through the window for the guard to see, hoping her supervisor hadn't yet gotten around to alerting the guards of her new status.

The guard glanced at the badge through the window and, when he lifted his key to unlock the door to allow her inside, she released the pent-up breath she held.

"Hi, I'm Dr. Ellie Crandall," she said, smiling up at the guard. "Don't suppose you know if Clarence MacArthur is still in?" she asked, flashing a purposeful smile on her face, hoping none of her anxiety showed.

The guard glanced down at his clipboard briefly, before looking back at her, shaking his head.

"'Fraid not, Dr. Crandall. Says here he left a bit ago. You just missed him," he said, shaking his head, his glance falling to the small portable television behind his desk.

Ellie put on a faux look of disappointment, hiding the relief she felt that Clarence wasn't around.

"Darn. Was hoping I'd catch him before he left for the day. I was supposed to give him something before he leaves town tomorrow."

"Well," the guard drawled, his eyes shifting to the television behind his desk before turning back to her.

"If you want you can go on up and put it on his desk. Said he'd be in tomorrow before he left for the airport," the guard supplied, and Ellie grinned.

"That would be great," she said and turned away.

She stopped, and turned back to the guard who was quickly walking back to his desk. She watched him pull out his chair, a grin of anticipation splitting his lined face as the theme music for *Judge Judy* blasted from the small set as a commercial ended. He rubbed his hands together gleefully, mumbling, "Oh, you 'bout to get it now, playa!"

"Oh, no…I didn't bring my key. Thought I'd catch him in time. Don't suppose you have the key?" she said, placing a sheepish look on her face, knowing the guard held the keys to all the offices.

She held her breath, hoping the lure of *Judge Judy* would prevent him from questioning her further. When he seemed to hesitate, his glance going to her and back to the television, Ellie rushed in to explain.

"It's just that I have a plane to catch myself tomorrow.

And if he doesn't get this…" She allowed her voice to trail away.

After a considering look he nodded his head. "Guess that wouldn't hurt anything. Here, why don't I give you the key. Just bring it back when you're finished," he said and Ellie hid a triumphant grin, sending a silent thank-you to Judge Judy.

"Just don't tell nobody," he said with a wink.

She grinned back. "I love *Judge Judy* myself," she said, and he laughed. "No fears…your secret is safe with me."

Before he could change his mind…or before Judge Judy could dispense her legendary swift judgment and end the show, Ellie grasped the key and swiftly strode toward the elevator, her heart bouncing against her chest in part jubilation and part anxiety.

Before unlocking the door to the office, Ellie peered though the glass pane of the small sitting area, just in case Clarence was inside, rapping her knuckles against the pane lightly. When she saw no sign of movement, no sound, she slipped the key in the lock and quickly walked inside.

After spending the last twenty minutes unable to find anything—no documents, no files, nothing to show Clarence's involvement in the photos—Ellie felt foolish, a cloud of despair cloaking her as she thought that maybe she'd been wrong after all and he hadn't been involved.

Which would mean that someone at Wilde had been, she thought, her shoulders slumping in dejection.

Putting her hands on her head, she allowed her head to droop.

"What did I think I would find?" With a sigh she bent

down to lift her bag from the floor where she'd placed it next to her.

As she did, she heard a slight ping and turned, glancing toward the computer.

She looked down and saw the message indicator on the left of the screen indicating a new email.

She'd opened the computer when she'd first sat down, surprised that he hadn't locked it, until she'd tried opening several documents only to find them password protected.

But, when the email alert pinged again, quickly she clicked on the icon, breathing out a huge sigh of relief when she was allowed in.

Her elation grew in direct proportion to the knot in her stomach, when after going though his inbox, she saw her name on several of the subject lines.

Ellie Crandall

The lump that had been slowly forming in her stomach grew and with shaky fingers she clicked on the first file folder with her name.

This email had only a single sentence, stating, *We got them*...along with an attachment. She clicked on the attachment and within moments a kaleidoscope of images filled the screen, the same ones that had been slipped beneath Shilah's door.

She drew in a breath. She'd never shown the photos to Clarence.

Chills ran over her spine as she opened the next document. In this one, Clarence had written to the USDA, telling them of Ellie's resignation, due to a family emergency.

A week before she'd told him about the pictures.

The last document was an email from Clarence to someone at Rolling Hills.

I've gotten rid of her, she won't stand in the way of our plans. Once the USDA finds out that it will take weeks to find another vet to take her place, they'll have no choice but to shut Wyoming Wilde down, and it's yours for the taking. I'll expect the usual arrangements, sent wireless to the same account this time tomorrow.

Like dominoes in her mind it all fell into place, and Ellie's hands fell to her stomach as it churned, making her literally sick as she thought of how stupid, how incredibly stupid she'd been. How could she have blamed Shilah, his family, for the duplicity?

She scanned the rest of the documents, her eyes widening at the deceit staring her in her face.

"You shouldn't have come here, Dr. Crandall."

Ellie spun around in her chair, her heart in her throat as she faced her supervisor. She glanced from his face to the .35 he held in his hand as he kicked the door closed and advanced into the room.

Chapter 26

Ellie's glance slid from Clarence, to the shiny .35 he held in his hand and back to meet his face. Swallowing deeply, she placed her printouts behind her back, trying to slip them into her purse without his noticing.

Dear God, what could she do...what could she say to him, she thought, racking her brains for a solution, anything to get her out of the office alive.

"I—I thought I'd catch you here, but I missed you." She swallowed, dragging a trembling smile to her face.

"Now, Ellie, surely you don't expect me to believe you just came here to shoot the breeze with me, did you?" he asked, walking inside the office and closing the door behind him. He reached behind his back and she heard a soft click as the lock slid into place.

Waiting for the fear to come, instead Ellie felt a steely

strength rush over her. Purposely putting on a disdainful expression, she turned to face him.

"Seems like someone's been a busy boy," she said, one side of her lip curling upward.

She saw the surprise in his eyes, as he halted in his steps momentarily.

Sensing she had a slight advantage, she turned back to her purse and withdrew the photos, she faced him again.

"Had you just come to me in the first place, all of this," she said, waving the photos in her hand, "wouldn't have been necessary, Clarence."

His glance slid to the photos in her hand, then back to her face. "Oh, really? And why is that?"

Firmly keeping a nonchalant smile in place she walked toward Clarence. Once she was close enough to him, she ran a finger down his chest, dropping her eyes.

"I'm sure we could have come to a…mutually satisfying…arrangement. It's still not too late for that, you know."

He frowned down at her, but she could sense his intrigue as well as the effect she was having on him, hiding her disgust at the way the front of his slacks bore evidence.

"And how's that?"

She shrugged, feigning calmness. "I'm guessing you were the one behind the pictures?" She went on, without waiting for his reply, "And…I'm guessing for whatever reason, you didn't want my report to go through. I'm also guessing the reason for that would be that you've made a side deal with someone who doesn't want the ranch cleared?"

She saw his face blanch.

"I'd say you're guessing way the hell too much," he said, eyes narrowing.

"Now, now… The report still hasn't been sent in. Think how much more effective…and immediate…it would be, if my report went in…doctored, of course."

"I'm listening," he said.

Playing it solely by ear, she went on, laughing lightly. "Appears to me you're going about this the hard way. Sure, you tell them my evidence was inconclusive, get my investigation thrown out, but that still leaves the problem of another investigator coming in. I have a feeling that after this the USDA will send in one of their own."

When he nodded his head, she went on. "But, like I said, if the report is sent in…altered, there would be no need for the USDA to continue with the investigation. And even if the Wildes protested the report, the damage would be done. They would be shut down and forced to sell."

He grabbed her hand, closing his fist around it so tightly for a moment that she turned pale. When he saw the reaction she couldn't hide, the ends of his lips curled up, the smile he gave her cruel.

"I never was one for playing games, Ellie." The warning in his voice made it clear what would happen if she were toying with him.

"Neither am I," she said, holding his gaze.

"So, what's in this for you?"

"I bet we can come up with an agreement that will make us both…happy," she said, allowing her lids to drop.

Ellie held her breath, her glance stealing to the gun

he still held in his hand, waiting for him to lower his guard, for just one minute…that's all she'd need.

She didn't think for a minute she still had a chance in hell that he'd just let her go after what she knew. But if he lowered his guard, and the gun, for just one minute, that's all the time she'd need.

He placed a finger beneath her chin, jerking her face up to meet his. Slowly he lowered his mouth to meet hers, and Ellie bit back the nausea that bubbled in her stomach. Right before his lips met hers, she reared back her knee, and with as much force as she could, rapped him in the groin.

With a curse he dropped the gun, grabbing his groin, and fell to his knee. Quickly scrambling away from him she spun around, searching for the gun. Knowing she had only a few precious moments, she lunged for the weapon. As she did so, she twisted her knee, the painful tear she heard nearly making her black out.

She pushed away the pain and, scrambling to her feet, crawled the short distance to reach the gun.

As her hands curled around it, she cried out in pain when Clarence landed on her hard, and together they rolled along the floor. With gritted teeth, Ellie held on to the gun, knowing her life was on the line.

For long moments nothing was heard in the room but their panting breath, as Ellie fought hard to maintain her hold on the weapon.

Her head snapped back and a cry fell from her lips when he reared his hand back and slapped her hard across the face, snatching the gun from her.

Tears fell from her eyes when he grabbed her and hauled her to her feet. The tears that ran down her face weren't from the pain, but an overwhelming sense of failure.

"Let's go," he panted, forcing her close to his side, turning to leave the office.

Shilah killed the lights on his truck, allowing the engine to idle as he glanced down at the slip of paper on the passenger seat. He'd been given the address of the building, the headquarters of the company Ellie worked for, by her father less than three hours ago. Driving like the proverbial bat out of hell, adrenaline racing through his veins, he'd made the three-hour drive in less than two.

With relief he saw Ellie's small Toyota in the isolated parking lot, he breathed a sigh of relief, drumming his hands impatiently against the steering wheel, deciding what his next move should be.

The day Ellie had shown him the damning photographs, he'd gone to his brothers. Although he hadn't shown them the photos, he'd told them what had transpired between them and grimly the brothers had spent the morning going over their next course of action in response to the blackmail.

A blackmail he and his brothers all agreed wasn't aimed at destroying Ellie, but the ranch. Mentally wrestling with the accusations she'd thrown at him, Shilah still hadn't been able to get her out of his mind or heart, as over the course of the next two days he and his brothers had questioned each of the men who worked for them. But none had shown any hint of deceit.

That morning two things had happened that led to his sitting in a truck, outside Jasper and Brant, deciding his next move.

Lilly had come to him and spoken of her concern about Anna, the new kitchen help she'd hired. Not in the mood to deal with domestic issues, he'd impatiently waved the concern to the side when Lilly told him she believed Anna was somehow involved.

Shilah, along with his brothers and Lilly, had gone to the girl's room and found her there, packing her bags, fear in her eyes.

They hadn't even had to ask to know she was guilty. Before they could speak, she'd taken one look at each of the big men crowding inside the small room before she'd broken down crying, admitting what she'd done.

With tears streaming down her face, she'd outlined her involvement in the scheme to discredit the ranch. A man who'd claimed to work for the USDA had approached her in town with an offer she hadn't been able to refuse.

The only thing she had to do was follow Ellie and report back to him anything she learned as she went about her investigation. When she'd seen Ellie and Shilah together, she'd told the man and he'd ordered her to follow them take pictures of them together. When she'd shared with him the pictures she'd then been told to place them under Shilah's door. And that was all she'd had to do.

Anna had cried as she'd finished admitting her guilt, saying she'd only done it because she needed the money for the baby she was carrying, that the father of her child had left her and she desperately needed the money.

Shilah had felt no sympathy for the woman, only a boiling rage at what she'd done.

He'd rushed to Ellie's parents' home to find Ellie and tell her what had happened. Once there, her father had met him at the door and refused to allow Shilah inside. He'd swallowed his pride and pleaded with her father. The elder Dr. Crandall's face had softened lightly, and with a sigh he'd told Shilah he had 2.2 minutes to tell what he could *possibly* say to allow him into his home.

Shilah had accomplished the task in half the time, humbly telling Ellie's father that he loved her.

Reluctantly her father had allowed him in. There he'd told Shilah that Ellie had driven to Cheyenne earlier that morning to talk to her supervisor. Shilah had stopped him, asking the name of her supervisor.

When he told him, Shilah's heart had all but stopped, recalling the name Anna had mentioned when Nate had asked her the name of the man who'd approached her.

Clarence MacArthur.

Shilah had spun around and run toward his truck, his tires leaving long skid marks in the street as he hastily flipped around and pushed his foot full down on the accelerator, rushing toward the highway and Ellie.

With shaky fingers he'd called the ranch and told Lilly what he'd learned, telling his brothers to meet him in Cheyenne. After getting off the phone with Lilly, he'd called Dr. Crandall, asking for the address.

Now, he cut the engine on the truck, pulling the keys from the ignition. As he opened his door, he jumped out, racing toward the entry. He had just reached the revolving door when a sound caught his attention and he turned, frowning.

Coming from the side entrance he saw two figures, one tall, thin, the other smaller, walking closely together. He would have kept walking had he not looked closer. The woman stumbled, and the man grabbed her by the arm, dragging her to her feet. Before Shilah could make a move, he saw the woman's foot sweep out in a arch, catching the man off guard, bringing him to his knees. At the last moment, before the man went down, he grabbed her by the waist, bringing her down with him.

A sick feeling nearly doubled Shilah over as realization hit who the couple were.

At the same time the couple rolled on the ground together, and the overhead beaming halogen light shone against the shiny chrome-plated handle of a .35.

His heart felt like it exploded from his chest as he took off at a run toward the couple, yelling Ellie's name.

His world came to a stumbling halt when, as if in slow motion he saw her lift her head toward the sound of his voice, and immediately the rat-a-tat sound of bullets rent the air.

Chapter 27

Ellie groaned and lifted her hand to her head, feeling as though a thousand little men were in her head beating a thousand little drums. She inhaled a whooshing breath, when her small movement escalated their evil beat until it felt as though her personal band had doubled their size.

When she tried to rise, the throbbing ache in her head rushed through her body, down to her knee, and she hissed in pain.

She opened her eyes, squinting against the bright light, and glanced around her. God, where was she?

She glanced down at herself and saw that a thin white cotton sheet covered her body as she lay on a narrow bed. Frowning, her eyes traveled around the room, her frown deepening as she took in the sterile white walls. Her glance landed on the stand next to her, where she saw an IV slowly dripping, the long thin tubes attached to her right arm.

She closed her eyes and again tried to rise, before dizziness swamped her, fleeting memories floating in and out of her mind.

"Ellie, baby, don't move, please, baby!"

She pried her eyes open at the sound of Shilah's voice and watched him stride toward her.

"Shilah?" she croaked out, as soon as he knelt down beside her. "Where am I?"

"I'm here, baby. I just stepped out for a minute to call your folks and tell them you're okay," he whispered, running a trembling hand over her hair.

"But where am I?" she asked, panic setting in when she couldn't remember where she was or why.

"Just lay back, baby, please. I'll explain."

She licked dry lips and nodded her head. She watched as he dragged a chair from a nearby wall, and stationing it close to her, sat down.

"You're at the medical center. You were shot," he said, taking her hand in his. "But, you're okay, baby.... Everything is going to be okay."

Ellie smiled weakly. "Seems we've done this before, huh?" she asked.

She felt his hand that was in her hair pause before he continued to stroke her head.

"Yeah, and just like before, it's my fault."

"Your fault?" she asked, as memories of what had happened filled her mind. "You didn't do any—"

He brought her hand to his lips. As she turned her head slightly, she saw a tortured look cross his handsome face.

"If I hadn't called your name when I did, you wouldn't have gotten shot," he stated, his face ravaged.

"Shilah," she whispered, the look on his face breaking her heart. "No, it wasn't your fault," she said, frowning as memories flashed in and out of her mind.

Taking her hand in his, his words halting, he filled her in on what had happened. After hearing the gunshots, he'd run and tackled Clarence, dragging him away from Ellie.

Shilah told her his brothers had been right behind him. Seeing what was going down, they had called the police the minute their feet hit the cement, running toward Shilah and Ellie.

Although only vaguely, she remembered Shilah holding her, tears streaming down his face as he cradled her in his arms, waiting for the ambulance and police to arrive. Nate and Holt had held an unconscious Clarence between the two of them.

As he spoke memories flooded her mind; Clarence's duplicity, their confrontation, Shilah running toward her, crying out her name.

"I'm so sorry, baby. Sorry you got shot, sorry I distracted you and you got shot…God, I'm so sorry," he said, his voice choked with emotion.

"I should be the one begging your forgiveness," she said, shaking her head, thinking of the cruel accusations she had hurled at him, accusations that had led to her going to Cheyenne.

"No, baby. I understand. You had every right to think what you did. And you were right, it was someone at the ranch," he said, and told her of Anna's involvement.

"So…what happens now?" Ellie asked, her voice hoarse.

"With what we know from Anna, the police will be brought in, along with the USDA."

Hearing that, Ellie bit the bottom of her lip, wondering what that meant for her, once the pictures were released.

He leaned down and kissed the frown away.

"No fears about your reputation, baby. With the information we have, they'll do a full investigation of Clarence, along with Rolling Hills. He'll be charged with blackmail and attempted fraud," he paused, a disgusted look crossing his handsome face. "Unfortunately, more than likely Rolling Hills will lay it all on the exec who was MacArthur's contact, make him the scapegoat and MacArthur will and get off. But at least the message will be sent to the bastards not to mess with the Wildes," he finished, a hard edge firming his jaw.

Shilah glanced down at her, his look softening. "Don't worry about any of that, right now, baby. None of that matters as much as you," he said, his voice breaking.

It dawned on Ellie just then how much he loved her.

"Remember when I told you I left home, because I got tired of people feeling sorry for me?"

"Yes, baby, I do…but please, don't talk. You've been through a lot, we can talk later," he said.

She shook her head and took a shallow breath. "No, let me get this out while I can," she said. "That wasn't it. I was running. Not from the looks of pity, or my parents' overbearing—loving, but overbearing—ways. It was because—" She stopped and closed her eyes.

"Are you in pain?" She felt him touch her hand. "Let me get the nurse, baby—"

"No," she opened her eyes, seeking his. "I—I'm fine." She took another breath and said in a rush, "I was running from you. From what I knew was there between us. I was scared, scared that how I felt about you...that you didn't feel the same way. I—I knew I couldn't hold it in anymore, the way I felt about you. And, I—I was afraid you would reject me," she said in one long rush.

"Baby—" His voice broke and Ellie saw his dark eyes shimmer with tears, and one lone tear escape down his lean cheek.

"I didn't want to see the same look in your eyes that I saw from other people. It would have killed me to see that. You meant too much to me for me to have been able to handle that."

"Ellie, don't you know how I feel? How long I've felt like this? How damn long I've loved you? God, woman, I could choke you right now if I didn't love you so damn much!"

"Wh...what?" Ellie said, torn between laughter and tears as he gently enfolded her in his arms.

He pulled away from her, thumbing a hand over her cheek, wiping away the tear that had escaped without her knowing.

"Thank you for loving me," he said simply, drawing her back into his arms. "Remember at the restaurant you told me you thought I was a good man?" he asked, and she nodded her head against his chest. She felt him draw in a deep, shuddering breath before he pulled away from her, settling her back on the bed.

"I know this probably isn't the best timing...the best time to ask you, but..." He allowed his sentence to trail away and she saw the deep breath he took, frowning as he rose, walking over to the corner of the room where his jacket lay over a small table. He lifted something from the pocket and walked back toward her.

He pushed the chair aside, and as he knelt down, Ellie felt her heart slam against her chest, her mouth opening, forming a perfect O. He brought her hand to his mouth, turned the palm over and kissed the center before holding it lightly in his, palm down.

"If you give me the chance, I'll do my best to prove I'm that man you think I am, Ellie, for the rest of our lives," he said, sliding a ring over her left finger. "Ellie, will you marry me?"

Unable to speak past the clog in her throat, Ellie bobbed her head up and down. She reached her arms out as he slowly, carefully enfolded her in his embrace. "Of course I'll marry you," she said, and held on tight as his arms closed around her.

Unashamedly, Ellie allowed the tears to run freely down her face, marveling at the way life and coincidence had brought them back together again, and love had forged an unbreakable bond between them that had broken down all other barriers.

* * * * *

Wilde IN WYOMING *Saddle Up...to a Wilde*

Kimberly Kaye Terry

invites you to discover
the Wilde brothers of Wyoming

Book #1
TO TEMPT A WILDE
On Sale February 22, 2011

Book #2
TO LOVE A WILDE
On Sale March 29, 2011

Book #3
TO DESIRE A WILDE
On Sale April 26, 2011

KIMANI™
ROMANCE

www.kimanipress.com

KPWIWSP

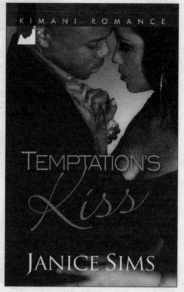

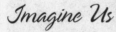

REQUEST YOUR FREE BOOKS!

2 FREE NOVELS
PLUS 2 FREE GIFTS!

KIMANI™
ROMANCE

Love's ultimate destination!

YES! Please send me 2 FREE Kimani™ Romance novels and my 2 FREE gifts (gifts are worth about $10). After receiving them, if I don't wish to receive any more books, I can return the shipping statement marked "cancel." If I don't cancel, I will receive 4 brand-new novels every month and be billed just $4.69 per book in the U.S. or $5.24 per book in Canada. That's a saving of at least 16% off the cover price. It's quite a bargain! Shipping and handling is just 50¢ per book in the U.S. and 75¢ per book in Canada.* I understand that accepting the 2 free books and gifts places me under no obligation to buy anything. I can always return a shipment and cancel at any time. Even if I never buy another book, the two free books and gifts are mine to keep forever.

168/368 XDN FDAT

Name	(PLEASE PRINT)

Address	Apt. #

City	State/Prov.	Zip/Postal Code

Signature (if under 18, a parent or guardian must sign)

Mail to the **Reader Service**:
IN U.S.A.: P.O. Box 1867, Buffalo, NY 14240-1867
IN CANADA: P.O. Box 609, Fort Erie, Ontario L2A 5X3

Not valid for current subscribers to Kimani Romance books.

Want to try two free books from another line?
Call 1-800-873-8635 or visit www.ReaderService.com.

* Terms and prices subject to change without notice. Prices do not include applicable taxes. Sales tax applicable in N.Y. Canadian residents will be charged applicable taxes. Offer not valid in Quebec. This offer is limited to one order per household. All orders subject to credit approval. Credit or debit balances in a customer's account(s) may be offset by any other outstanding balance owed by or to the customer. Please allow 4 to 6 weeks for delivery. Offer available while quantities last.

Your Privacy—The Reader Service is committed to protecting your privacy. Our Privacy Policy is available online at www.ReaderService.com or upon request from the Reader Service.

We make a portion of our mailing list available to reputable third parties that offer products we believe may interest you. If you prefer that we not exchange your name with third parties, or if you wish to clarify or modify your communication preferences, please visit us at www.ReaderService.com/consumerschoice or write to us at Reader Service Preference Service, P.O. Box 9062, Buffalo, NY 14269. Include your complete name and address.

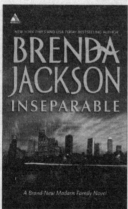